14/5/24

Please return on or before the latest date above.
You can renew online at *www.kent.gov.uk/libs*
or by telephone 08458 247 200

MORTAL PROSE

When a mogul of the literary world is murdered, D.I. Casey Clunes is on the case — though the victim's unpopularity ensures no shortage of suspects . . . Isobel is an intelligent woman — except when it comes to her new toyboy. Still, their relationship couldn't harm anyone else — or could it . . . ? The audience gasps as the new portrait of the headmaster of St Martin's is publicly revealed — defaced — followed by news that the headmaster himself has been shot dead by an unknown assailant . . . Three stories of mystery and murder from the pen of Geraldine Ryan.

Books by Geraldine Ryan
in the Linford Mystery Library:

LEAVE OVER
CURTAIN CALL
CASEY CLUNES INVESTIGATES
AN INSPECTOR CALLS
A STORM IN A TEACUP
SCHOOL FOR SCANDAL

GERALDINE RYAN

◆

MORTAL PROSE

Complete and Unabridged

LINFORD
Leicester

First published in Great Britain

First Linford Edition
published 2014

A catalogue record for this book is available
from the British Library.

ISBN 978–1–4448–2051–5

Published by
F. A. Thorpe (Publishing)
Anstey, Leicestershire

Set by Words & Graphics Ltd.
Anstey, Leicestershire
Printed and bound in Great Britain by
T. J. International Ltd., Padstow, Cornwall

This book is printed on acid-free paper

Contents

Mortal Prose

The thought of writing a book had never entered Casey's head. These days, mainly thanks to Finlay, she could barely even call herself a reader. So to say she was out of her comfort zone right now was a massive understatement.

This particular session was entitled 'How To Get a Publishing Deal'. It was the most prestigious event of the first ever Brockhaven Lit Fest and she'd been lucky to get a ticket. It involved a panel of literary big shots spouting advice on the subject to an auditorium of mostly women and a few men, feverishly taking notes or hugging their manuscripts to their chests like precious babies, all desperate to discover the secret of literary success.

Casey sat in the middle of the front row, wedged between a fidgety young woman with lank hair to her left and a man who, from his size, possessed a very distant relationship with the salad bar. She was here for Dom because she knew he'd never come to anything like this himself for fear of being rumbled. Not that she hadn't rumbled him already. She was a detective inspector, wasn't she? He was writing a novel. And he was keeping it a secret because he thought she'd see it as a bit of a flaky pastime for a grown man.

Maybe she did, but if Dom saw himself as a writer of fiction instead of the journalist he was, then the least she could do was encourage him. Writing was an industry just like anything else; hadn't literary agent Morris Greenwood just said so not two minutes ago? Wasn't he still banging on about it now? And if that was the case, she would sit here with everyone else, listen hard and suck up all the advice offered, so that when the day came that Dom felt able to show her his finished manuscript she'd have something a bit more constructive to offer than, 'Very nice dear.'

Morris Greenwood really ought to give his fellow panel members a turn, Casey thought. Time was running out and there was meant to be a Q&A session at the end. At this rate they'd never get to it. What was wrong with him? Right from the outset he'd done most of the talking, but for the last ten minutes or so he'd completely taken over, tripping over his words as if he couldn't get them out fast enough; and he had a glassy-eyed look about him she was beginning to find slightly alarming.

Zoë Steel, who'd organised the lit fest and who was acting as chair, looked thoroughly miserable at the way it was turning out. Instead of a well-mannered display of turn-taking, she'd got a megalomaniac and three extremely dissatisfied panellists on her hands, because they couldn't get a word in edgeways.

'Can I just say, Morris . . . ' No, the nervous young man sitting to the left of him could *not* say, because Morris wouldn't let him.

'While we're talking about the presentation of your manuscript, I should stress . . . ' he jabbered.

The distinguished-looking editor sitting

to his right and the nervous young man, a buyer for a well-known book chain apparently — which surprised Casey, given that he only looked about thirteen — exchanged mutinous glances. Whereupon the only other female on the panel beside Zoë Steel, newly published author Flora Curtiss, laid a gentle yet restraining hand on Morris and whispered something in his ear. It shut him up for about three seconds, long enough for Zoë Steel, cheeks flushed with mounting anxiety, to leap to her feet and declare this bit of the proceedings at a close.

'I really think we ought to throw the floor open now, Morris, if you don't mind,' she squeaked into her microphone. 'I'm sure the audience has lots of questions.'

Her suggestion was accompanied by 'hear, hear's from the panel as well as several from the audience, who'd been growing increasingly restless.

'But before I stop I would just like to mention the importance of . . . '

'Darling, *please*.'

Flora Curtiss's words couldn't have

been audible to anyone beyond the front row. Morris Greenwood turned to her and gave her a look of bewilderment. It was as if, thought Casey, he'd suddenly woken up sitting next to her and found himself in this room full of people with no idea of how he'd got there.

'It's hot in here, isn't it?' He was speaking just to her now, completely oblivious of hands waving in the air hoping Zoë might pick them to ask a question.

Casey sat forward in her seat. Something wasn't right with Morris Greenwood. He'd stopped talking at last, which was a blessing. But now he was sweating profusely, and his whole complexion had turned a waxy grey. She watched him struggle to his feet and begin to tug at his tie as if desperate for air.

It was all over in moments, before either audience or panel had fully registered what they were witnessing. Clutching dramatically at his heart in the manner of a rather bad amateur actor, Morris Greenwood let out a low moan, before tumbling to the ground, silent at last.

Two weeks previously

'He wanted *what*?' Dom paused in his task of mixing spaghetti with bolognese sauce for Finlay's supper and glanced up at Casey, who was hoisting their son into his high chair.

'Tickets. For the Lit Fest. For his wife.' Casey rolled up her son's sleeves and set about swathing him in an extra-large bib. Finlay could get extremely enthusiastic about spaghetti bolognese. 'The boss's wife is mad on some new writer, apparently, but she can't get tickets to hear her talk about her novel for love or money. McGovern thought I might have some inside connections. Being as you're going to be performing.'

'Oh, God, please don't remind me!' Dom attacked Finlay's supper so vigorously with his mixing spoon that a dollop of the sauce flew up from the bowl and landed on his T-shirt. Another one for the rollerball, thought Casey with a sigh.

'I thought he'd sent for me to give me a

dressing down,' she went on. 'That thief got away with another three wallets and two purses last week. So of course it's all my fault for failing to be in five places at once.'

She was determined this conversation was not going to turn into a repetition of the one they'd been having nightly, ever since Dom revealed he'd been invited to talk about his book. *By-lines and Deadlines*, it was called, a collection of amusing articles about his years as a junior reporter on a rural daily newspaper long since defunct. He'd worked hard on it and it had paid off, earning him a publisher, a modest advance and this slot at the Lit Fest.

Dom was convinced he'd bitten off more than he could chew, and since the invitation not a day had passed without him voicing his conviction that he was going to make an ass of himself. Dutifully she'd played the wifely role, telling him he'd be fine and that there was nothing to worry about. But her reassurances had fallen on deaf ears.

It was a real struggle for Casey to bite

her tongue. It was one hour in front of an audience who'd paid to see him because they'd read his book and enjoyed it, she longed to say. There would be applause, and laughter, and lots of gushing from fans collaring him afterwards and asking him to sign their copies.

He should try doing a turn in front of a crowd of snarling residents at the community centre on the Halewood Estate, who thought that she, as a representative of Brockhaven's police force, was totally useless and cared more about the rights of criminals than the rights of victims.

To be fair to him, he'd reined in the self-pity a bit recently. But give him the slightest opportunity to bring it up again and — just as he was doing now — he'd wrestle the subject of any conversation they were having away from her and put this one in its place. Well, tonight she wasn't having any.

'The Brockhaven Bag Snatcher strikes again.' Dom, done with mashing up Finlay's meal, set about serving up the grown-up portions.

'The *what?*' Casey considered the

phrase disdainfully.

'That's what the *Gazette* are calling the thief.'

Casey snorted. She had nothing but contempt for the *Brockhaven Gazette*, who had never let the facts get in the way of a good story. 'Typical,' she said. 'First of all, whoever's doing this isn't interested in bags; and second of all, they don't discriminate. He's nicked just as many wallets as purses.'

''Bags' provides that bit of alliteration that all sub-editors love,' Dom said. 'And 'wallets' is too many letters, I guess.'

'Well you'd know all about that, wouldn't you?' Casey said. 'All those years you spent working on that rag.'

'Hey, don't call it a rag.' Dom pretended to be offended. 'I have very fond memories of the *Brockhaven Gazette*.'

Finlay squealed delightedly, kicking his legs as Dom set his bowl of pasta before him. 'Sketti! Sketti!' he cried.

Casey, handing him his spoon, gazed at her son fondly and told him to tuck in. She considered Dom's words. It had been his habit of skulking in the shadows

11

waiting for Casey — then a mere detective constable — in the vain hope she might pass on the juicy details of whatever investigation she was working on at the time that had eventually brought them together. How long ago was that now? Four years? In the immortal words of Samuel Goldwyn, they'd all passed a lot of water since then.

'I suppose it was good for something,' she grudgingly agreed as she took her steaming plate from Dom. 'Mmm! Smells good!'

Dom nodded graciously and began to heap mounds of Parmesan all over his plate, a habit that drove Casey to despair. 'Anyway, who's this writer Mrs McGovern's so desperate to see?'

'Flora Somebody-or-other,' she said. 'Doesn't mean anything to me.'

'Flora Curtiss. The latest in the Curtiss dynasty. She's from a huge writing dynasty so it's hardly surprising she's followed in the family profession. On top of that she's young, beautiful, clever and up for an award for her first book.'

Casey held out her hand for the

Parmesan in the faint hope there was some left. 'Beautiful, talented *and* privileged. I hate her already,' she said, po-faced. 'Is she single?'

'Apparently she's in a relationship with her agent. He's years older than her. He's coming to the festival too, to sit on a panel with her and a couple of other literary types — editors, publishers, that sort of thing. 'How to Get a Publishing Deal,' the sessions's called.'

Casey wound a length of spaghetti round her fork, and waited for him to say more. But he'd already turned his attention to his meal, so she did the same. It tasted as good as it looked, she decided. Dom really was getting to be an excellent cook since he'd embarked on his sabbatical to write his little book. She quickly checked herself. She really must stop calling it his 'little book'. It wasn't any littler than any other book really. 'How do you know all this stuff? About this Flora Curtiss's love life, I mean,' Casey said, when she'd almost finished.

'The *Gazette* again,' Dom said. 'They just did an interview with her.'

'Must be nice to have time to read the paper during the day.' She smiled at him affectionately across the table to show she meant no malice. It suited her, Dom being at home. It meant she didn't have to run home for the nanny and she could relax knowing that Finlay was getting plenty of male attention, which she was convinced every little boy needed.

'All gone!' Casey and Dom turned their eyes towards Finlay, who'd tipped his bowl upside-down to prove — in case there was any doubt — that he had indeed got to the end of his meal in seconds flat. The fact that he was wearing a great deal of it over his face and hair didn't alter Casey's conviction that beneath it all he was still the most beautiful baby ever born. And she wasn't just saying that because she was his mother. Dom thought so too; she could see it in his face.

'Bath time, I think,' she said. 'Agreed?'

'Alternatively, I could put the garden hose on him,' Dom said, with a grin.

★　★　★

14

Meanwhile, Daisy Bannister tossed her copy of the *Brockhaven Gazette* onto the conservatory floor. The sun's rays, still warm, transformed her cat Chubbins into a burning bush of orange. As the newspaper landed on the cracked tiles, he glanced up from fastidiously washing his bottom to glare at it.

'How in God's name did he do it, Chubbins?' She reached for the small sherry she'd poured earlier — her usual reward at the end of her writing day — and tossed it back in one gulp. She needed another one, and quickly. 'That girl is young enough to be his daughter.' Unable to stop herself, she picked up the paper and read the words again: 'Latest in Curtiss Dynasty Publishes Sure-Fire Best Seller', ran the headlines, below which was a half-page photo of a rather stunning young woman. Daisy allowed her gaze to sweep over the perfect features: that smooth brow, the swan-like neck, the trim figure, and that hair — blonde, abundant and dishevelled. Not in the same way her own hair was dishevelled after a morning spent weeding, but in a manner that

15

suggested great attention and expense had been lavished upon it. 'Bed head hair', she'd heard it called, which suggested all sorts of delights she'd personally been starved of for a good few years now. Since Morris, in fact. She shuddered.

Why hadn't she thought to ask who else would be appearing at the festival before she'd signed that damned contract? Well, she knew why. She guessed people in the village thought she was well-off — after all, her picture books still sold well enough. But the world of publishing had become a cut-throat one over the years. Her advances had shrunk to a mere pittance; and as for royalties . . . well, the less said about those the better.

She couldn't get out of it now. But how on earth was she supposed to behave if she bumped into Morris and his new paramour? Brockhaven was a small town and the chances of them missing each other were slim indeed.

'Ruddy man,' she whispered. 'How dare he flaunt another woman in my face? How *dare* he?'

She realised she'd somehow managed to unpick the loose stitching from the arm of her chair, and swore loudly. She could ill afford a new suite the way things were at the moment.

Chubbins, perhaps sensing her darkening mood, leaped onto her lap and began to nuzzle her, purring rapturously.

'If he thinks he's going to get away with it he's got another thing coming,' she whispered softly into his silken ear.

★ ★ ★

'I'm afraid that although the crash team tried to resuscitate the patient with CPR followed by defibrillation, he failed to respond to our efforts and was pronounced dead at 15.03.'

Casey, who'd taken Flora Curtiss's arm immediately when she realised that the white-coated doctor coming through the doors was heading their way, felt the young woman's body sag as a pitiful sob escaped her.

From his manner of addressing Casey, rather than Flora, it became apparent that the doctor had made the assumption that

Morris Greenwood was — or rather had been — *her* partner, not Flora's. Given that Flora looked about twenty-five and nearer the age of the newly deceased's daughter, it was an easy mistake to make.

'Look,' she said, putting him right. 'I'm D.I. Casey Clunes from the Brockhaven Constabulary. This is Flora Curtiss, Mr Greenwood's — er — friend.'

The doctor's eyes flicked sideways and registered Flora, whose face was now awash with tears. Even in grief she looked beautiful.

'I see,' he said, not missing a beat. 'Would you like to see him?'

'No,' she sobbed. 'I mean yes. I probably should.'

'You don't have to, Flora,' Casey said gently. Then she turned to the doctor. 'Look,' she said. 'This is obviously a terrible shock. Is there somewhere private we can take Miss Curtiss? To get a cup of tea, even?'

'Of course. I was about to suggest.' His face took on a cautious expression. 'There are things I'd like — I need — to discuss with Miss Curtiss, if she feels up to it. My room perhaps.'

18

Once in Dr Brealey's office, Flora Curtiss shook her head in refusal at the polystyrene mug of pale liquid Casey held out to her. Casey, intrigued to find out what exactly Dr Brealey felt the needed to discuss with Flora, didn't want to waste any more time on niceties and decided not to press it.

'Do you know if Mr Greenwood was a drug user. Miss Curtiss?'

Casey sat up straight when she heard the question. Earlier, watching Morris Greenwood moving jerkily and struggling to make sense of the stream of words that rushed from his lips, the same question had occurred to her, but she'd dismissed it out of hand. She'd seen kids behaving in this self-same way, strung out on Dexys. But men of fifty-five don't take speed, she'd told herself. They drank red wine and spirits and only took tablets to control their blood pressure and their bladders.

Bewilderment flickered across Flora's face. 'Drugs? Of course not,' she said. 'Morris had a heart condition. It was quite serious. The only tablets he took were for that.' Glancing at Casey for confirmation, she added, 'But I told them that in the ambulance.'

Casey confirmed her statement. 'Are you saying you found other drugs in his blood stream, Doctor?' she added.

'We found traces of amphetamine, yes.'

'That would explain his odd behaviour, I guess,' said Casey. The doctor gave her a quizzical look. 'He was hyped up. Sweating. Gabbling. I've seen it before,' Casey said. Drugs . . . she hated them, and what they did to people.

'He was acting strangely, you're right,' Flora said. 'Everyone noticed it.'

'Had he been drinking too?'

Flora shrugged. 'A little wine at the buffet lunch prior to the session,' she said, and added apologetically, 'Morris gets a little nervous before speaking publicly. He's a shy man at heart. Was, I mean,' she added, after a pause.

'That could explain it,' the doctor said. 'Mixing amphetemines with medication for the heart,then adding alcohol, can be a lethal cocktail.'

'But Morris didn't take drugs. I told

you,' protested his girlfriend. 'Only prescription ones.'

Casey and Doctor Brealey exchanged glances. Casey guessed he was thinking exactly the same thing as she was. That couples had always kept secrets from each other since time immemorial, and maybe there were some things that Flora Curtess just didn't know about Morris Greenwood.

'The only way he would have taken these amphetemines would have been if someone slipped them in his drink,' Flora went on.

'And who do you think might want to do that?'

'It's obvious. That dreadful Scot, Fraser Cross, one of Morris's writers. He was at the buffet, piling as much free food onto his plate as he could manager.' Flora plucked nervously at a strand of hair. 'A couple of months ago, Morris told him he could no longer represent him.'

'Did he give a reason?'

'He gave two, actually. One, no one was reading Fraser's published novels any more; and two, he'd read the latest manuscript and didn't think he could sell it.'

Ouch, thought Casey.

'I was on my way up to see him — Morris, I mean. Morris was at the door saying something about how much he'd enjoyed working with Fraser and how he hoped they could part as friends. A complete gentleman, as always,' she said, before Casey could suggest otherwise. 'But Fraser went ballistic. Started swearing and calling Morris all the names under the sun.'

'But did he actually threaten Morris?'

'Yes. He did. He told Morris that he wasn't going to get away with dumping him.' Flora Curtiss bit her bottom lip. 'And then he said, 'You'd better watch your back if you know what's good for you.' I heard him, Inspector. So what are you going to do about it?'

★ ★ ★

'He did what?'

Casey glanced from one officer to the other, wondering which was the biggest chump — PC Will Doughty, fresh from being puppy-walked, or WPC Leila

22

Rasheed, who'd transferred from the Met to be nearer her fiancé, an extremely dubious motive in Casey's book. Didn't she trust the guy or something?

'Fraser Cross did a runner, Inspector. And we lost him.' At least WPC Rasheed had the good grace to hang her head.

Loyally, PC Doughty ploughed in to back her up. 'He just took off,' he said. 'It took us both by surprise.'

WPC Rasheed nodded in agreement. 'We followed him but the crowds slowed us down.'

'We think he hoped on a bus,' PC Doughty said. 'Going to Lowestoft.'

'So we alerted them that end.'

'And of course that's where he got off, am I right? At the bus station? Right in front of the cop car? And now he's safely under lock and key waiting to be interviewed?'

No answer was necessary. PC Doughty's red face and WPC Rasheed's refusal to remove her eyes from the floor said enough.

'Go and get your break, you two. You look knackered.' She was annoyed they hadn't managed to bring in Fraser Cross, but there was no pleasure to be had from bullying her inferiors. She much preferred to get stuck in with those above her in the pecking order. McGovern, for example. Oh, he was going to love this.

★ ★ ★

'It's really not as bad it looks, sir.' Casey scanned McGovern's desk. Amongst the heaps of files and the detritus of his lunch was a new photo. Mrs McGovern's idea, Casey suspected. It was a Happy Families one — McGovern looking distinctly shifty, his wife all smiles, and their two children: one sullen-faced teenage girl with a nose ring, and one grinning boy with his two front teeth missing. Quite cute really. It was almost impossible to believe that one day she'd have a pic of Finlay at the gap-toothed stage.

'And how do you make that out, exactly? You told me yourself that Fraser Cross had form for assault.'

'Well, that was a long time ago,' Casey hedged. 'Back in Glasgow.'

'You're right,' McGovern said. 'Probably

some pub brawl on a Saturday night.'

Casey pretended she hadn't heard. She often wondered if McGovern had ever actually attended a course on racial stereotyping or if he'd just ticked the box and claimed the expenses.

'Look. This is taking a risk, I know, but we only have Flora Curtiss's word that Morris Greenwood wasn't a regular user of speed. And that Fraser Cross threatened him that day at his office.'

Before she could finish, McGovern butted in. 'A man with a heart condition like his doesn't mix his medications, Casey. Not if he's just got himself a pretty young girlfriend half his age.'

Casey saw the logic in that.

'Besides, if he was innocent, why would he run away when approached by the police?'

'I don't know. But we can't condemn a man just on one person's say-so. Not without solid evidence.' Casey floundered around for something else to add and finally hit on it. 'You know, it could just as easily been Flora Curtiss who slipped him the pills. Maybe she told him they were herbal — something to calm his nerves before he got up on stage to face the literati of Brockhaven.'

McGovern sent her a withering look.

'Sir, Fraser Cross is down to do a workshop at the Lit Fest tomorrow, and that's why it doesn't matter so much that he's scarpered,' she said, refusing to be knocked off course. 'We can pick him up after that. Then if he doesn't bother to turn up for it, we'll know he's dodgy and we can put out a warrant for his arrest.'

'I suppose so,' McGovern said grudgingly.

'So, will that be all then, sir?'

'Yes. We're done here.' McGovern made his way to his desk with the purposeful stride of a man already onto the next thing. 'How did Dom's thing go, by the way?' he said over his shoulder as he began to sort through an open file.

Casey froze. *By-lines and Deadlines*. Dom's reading for his book. And she'd gone and missed it. He would never forgive her!

'Er — fine, sir,' she said, already creeping towards the door and wondering how on earth she was going to make it up to him.

McGovern made a half turn. 'So you never actually made it then?' he said over his shoulder.

★ ★ ★

There were six texts on Casey's phone: five from Dom and one from Debbie, the nanny. Dom's was the first.

Just setting off to give my talk. Hoping for a small earthquake.

Hi, Casey. Don't rush back. Finlay and me have got the day planned.

*Arrived at venue. Some punters here already. *gulps* Don't sit too close to front.*

Can't see you anywhere. Starts in five minutes.

Went quite well actually. Am guessing work got in way.

Back home. Debbie left. Finlay in bed. When you have a minute give us a ring and let me know when you'll be back.

Casey traced Dom's journey from belief to resignation through his texts. She envisaged him setting out, full of trepidation, but perhaps gleaning some comfort from the fact that she'd assured him she'd be there to support him. Then, as the minutes ticked by and it began to sink in that she wasn't going to make it, she imagined his disappointment. Poor Dom! She didn't think he'd ever spoken in front of an audience before. Usually it was just him and a laptop.

He must hate her right now. Frantically, she scrawled back over his messages, as if she needed to punish herself for her thoughtlessness. What, exactly, did 'it went quite well' mean? It went quite well and the organiser told me afterwards that it really didn't matter about me getting so tongue-tied? It went quite well even though only six people turned up?

It was no use. She was going to have to ring Dom and find out.

'Casey? Where are you?'

'Never mind about me. What about you?'

'What about me?'

Honestly, the man could be so infuriating! 'Your talk. I missed it. I'm so *so* sorry. How did it go? I mean, I got your text but

28

really, how did it go?'

'Oh, *that!* God, I can't believe I got myself into such a state about it. People enjoyed it. *I* even enjoyed it — once I knew you weren't coming.'

'You what?' Casey did a mental double take. 'You mean you never really wanted me there in the first place?'

'You would have made me nervous, Casey,' Dom said.

'Oh, Dom.' Why hadn't she thought he might feel that way about her being there? Honestly, sometimes she could be such a numpty.

'You're such a pro and I'm just a beginner when it comes to public speaking,' Dom said. 'I wouldn't have been able to concentrate if you'd been there.'

'Honestly, Dom.' Casey's voice flooded with relief. 'You're such a numpty.'

'Plus I wouldn't have been able to flirt with the audience, most of whom were women, if you'd been there,' he added mischievously.

'Dom!'

'Just keeping you on our toes!' Dom chucked. 'So, when can Finlay and I expect the pleasure of your company?' he added.

'I don't know. You've heard about Morris Greenwood, I'm guessing?' She had no doubt that news of his dramatic demise would be all over the town by now.

'Sure. It's awful news. But how is it a police matter?' Dom wanted to know. 'I read he'd suffered heart problems for a long time.' Casey paused long enough for Dom to rethink this assumption. 'Are you suggesting Morris Greenwood may have been murdered?'

'We can't say yet. There'll have to be an autopsy. But between you and me it's looking very suspicious. There was evidence of amphetamines in his blood.'

Dom gave a low whistle.

'Anyway, I kind of thought I'd pop back to the hospital. Have another word with Flora Curtiss.

'Is she a suspect?'

'I don't know,' she said guardedly. 'But there's no harm in having a chat with her, is there?'

★ ★ ★

Flora Curtiss didn't appear to have moved since Casey had left her a couple of hours previously. She was waiting for Morris's things, she told Casey from her seat in the relatives' room, but there'd been some sort of hold up. Casey sat down next to her. Had she noticed anything unusual about Morris's behaviour before he went on stage, she wanted to know,

'No, not really. He was looking forward to the event. But when he got up on stage it was like he'd forgotten what he was doing there. He was wild-eyed, twitchy, babbling his words.'

'And you're certain that in all the time you knew Mr Greenwood that he'd never taken amphetamines?'

'Of course not! Do you think I wouldn't have noticed?'

'As a matter of interest,' Casey went on, 'how long were you and Mr Greenwood in a relationship?'

'Depends by what you mean by *relationship*, Inspector.' Flora Curtiss was

31

calm again. 'As a couple we were together three months. But our working relationship began nine months ago, when Morris replied to my enquiry email.'

Casey knew about enquiry emails. It was one of the few useful tips she'd picked up from Morris before he'd gone off-piste. 'So he liked your synopsis and asked to read your novel?'

'He got back to me within a week. Invited me in for a meeting and signed me on the spot.' She leaned forward to take a sip of water. 'I was very lucky, I suppose.'

Some would have said Morris Greenwood had been the lucky one.

'Have you spoken to Fraser Cross yet and confronted him about those threats he made to Morris?' Flora and swapped her misty-eyed gaze for a stern look.

'You sound like my boss,' Casey said, deftly sidestepping the question.

'I've always wondered about writing a crime novel,' Flora replied. 'I expect your boss is a monster with a heart of gold. They usually are in crime novels.'

'Not my boss,' Casey said. 'He doesn't

even possess a heart — gold or otherwise.' She leaned forward in her seat. 'But to get back to the buffet. You said you saw Fraser Cross there. Did he approach Morris at all? Could he, for instance, have slipped something into his drink?'

'I didn't see him with Morris,' she admitted. 'But it doesn't mean he didn't approach him. There were lots of people milling around.'

'So Morris was on his own for some of the time?'

'If you mean on his own without me, then yes,' she said. 'But whenever I glanced his way he always seemed to be deep in some conversation with one person or another.'

'Can you remember any names?'

'That ditsy woman who writes and illustrates the children's books. Daisy Somebody-or-other — she spoke to him.'

'You mean Daisy Bannister?'

Finlay adored Daisy Bannister books. There was a whole series about a cat called Chubbins, who always got into loads of trouble but miraculously managed to get out of it again. A bit like

Finlay, now she came to think of it. Perhaps she should go and have a chat with her, and take some of Finlay's books for her to sign. Take Finlay even.

'And the organiser was there. Zoe Steele.'

Casey nodded.

'And of course there were the aspiring writers, all tripping up over each other and wondering why he hadn't pulled their novel from the slush pile and recognised it for the masterpiece it was.'

It was all right having talent, Casey thought. But to belittle those without was cruel and unnecessary.

Flora sighed. 'I don't suppose any of that is much help in catching a killer, is it, Inspector? I mean, who's going to slip someone pills in the middle of a busy reception? If it were me I'd do it somewhere private.'

Casey smiled. There was a knock on the door.

'Oh, goodness!' Flora Curtiss put her fingers to her lips. 'I didn't mean . . . I hope you don't suspect me of killing Morris!' She let out a peal of laughter.

'I'll just get that,' Casey said. Was she imagining it, or was Flora Curtiss rattled?

Outside the door was WPC Rasheed. She was carrying a clear plastic bag which appeared to contain items of clothes.

'Leila! What a pleasure,' Casey said.

WPC Rasheed smiled nervously. 'They said you were here,' she said. 'You might be interested in looking through the deceased's belongings.'

Casey took the bag from Leila. It crackled in her hands. 'What am I looking for exactly?'

'Well, it was my fiancé who told me. He bagged them up. The belongings. He was going to given them to Miss Curtiss, being as how they were — you know . . . '

Casey did know.

'But when he looked inside the man's wallet he found one of those donor cards and that's when he knew he couldn't give the stuff to her.'

Casey waited.

'There was space there for the name of the next of kin. And when I read whose name was there I thought it might be important. Because she's at the Lit Fest too. I've seen her in the brochure.'

'Who is it, Leila? Who are you referring to as Morris Greenwood's next of kin?'

WPC Leila Rasheed fixed Casey with her deep brown eyes. 'Daisy Bannister,' she said. 'Seems like she's his wife.'

★   ★   ★

'Chubbins! Chubbins!'

The cardboard cut-out of the ginger cat was taller than Finlay by a head and far too wide for him to get his chubby embrace around. As soon as he'd spotted it in the foyer of the Brougton Hotel, in the spot allocated to Daisy Bannister for her book signing, he'd torn himself away from Dom and Casey and gone hurtling towards it.

Now he was lost among a sea of legs, and completely out of hearing somewhere in the small but determined higgledy-piggledy smattering of Daisy Bannister fans, old and young, that still remained.

'Shall I just see if I can grab myself a coffee somewhere while you stand in the queue with Finlay?' Dom asked. 'Providing we ever find him again in this melee, that is?'

'Nice try, sweetie pie.' Casey swapped the six well-thumbed Daisy Bannister books she was carrying to her other side. 'Look. He's over there. I recognise his trainers. You grab him. I'll save us a place in the queue.'

Dom hated Daisy Bannister books. Too black and white, he always grumbled, whenever Finlay clamoured for Chubbins at story time. But Casey disagreed. In her job there was very little white, and the black often got away scot-free, which left her the palette of murky greys to deal with. A bit of Daisy Bannister of an evening went a long way to fooling her that the world was essentially a good place. Even if the feeling only lasted as long it took to get to the end of the story.

They'd decided to come to the book signing on a whim and had got here in the nick of time, according to one of the Lit Fest volunteers who told them that the crowd had shrunk considerably since Daisy Bannister had first taken her seat. It was Casey's day off and she needn't have been there at all — Finlay had absolutely no idea who Daisy Bannister was, and if she had graced his copies of her picture books with her signature he wouldn't have been able to read it anyway.

He loved Chubbins though. And it was an opportunity to get a glimpse of the woman who, however briefly, had been married to Morris Greenwood and to sniff out whether she had anything to hide. A little chat in an informal situation would help her decide where to go next.

There was another reason too. Fraser Cross ought to be giving his workshop in Room 201 round about now. She'd been informed that towards the end of the session, two officers would have positioned themselves outside the door, their intention being to ask him to accompany them to the station for a second time. Casey was keen to see whether he'd go quietly this time, and down here on the ground floor she'd get a good view. If he refused, then they needed to get some hard evidence so they could arrest him. If he complied, well, she was well placed to accompany him and do the interview. Especially as Dom was so near to hand, so she wouldn't have to worry about what to do with Finlay. Where was that boy, by the way?

The queue moved forward quickly. Casey surmised that Daisy Bannister had had years of experience at this sort of thing and had perfected her signature and her patter. She was quite happy to chat to the children, most of whom barely reached her eye line, but she had no compunction about cutting off the gushing mums mid-flow.

By the time Casey had reached the head of the queue there was still no sign of Dom and Finlay. Neither was there anyone queuing behind her to whom she could relinquish her place while she went to look for them.

'Oh!' Daisy Bannister peered over her rimless glasses at Casey, looking slightly bemused. 'No youngster to proffer?'

'I seem to have lost him,' Casey said. 'But I've got his books.'

Daisy Bannister was already on the first one, pen hovering.

'Name?' she said.

Perhaps Casey should have been more understanding. After all, it had clearly been a long and arduous session and the woman was getting on in years, even though the shade of her hair would have made Goldilocks look like a dirty blonde.

'Casey Clunes. Actually, I'm a police officer,' she said.

The pen hovered over the page. 'And what can I do to help you, Officer?' she said. 'I'm more than happy to donate some of my books for your Christmas raffle.'

'That would be very kind,' Casey said. 'But actually I'd like to ask you about Morris Greenwood. And your relation-ship with him.'

With slow deliberation, Daisy Bannister screwed the lid of her pen on tight and placed it on the desk. 'My relationship with Morris Greenwood ended in 1992, Officer,' she said.

'But you were married to him, weren't you?' From her jacket pocket she removed the kidney donor card that WPC Leila Rasheed's boyfriend, the nurse, had found when he'd been in the process of bagging up the dead man's belongings.

Daisy Bannister gave the card no more than a cursory glance. 'I can't deny it,' she said. Then, raising her eyes to meet

Casey's, she asked, 'Is it relevant?'

Casey shrugged. 'You tell me, Ms Bannister,' she said. 'You were seen talking to Mr Greenwood just minutes before he collapsed and died. Later, it was discovered that there were amphetamines in his blood stream. No one can explain how they got there and why he would have taken them. But they definitely resulted in his death'

What happened next took the whole room by surprise. Casey, alerted by sudden shouts and squeals, turned as Fraser Cross came running down the wide staircase hell for leather with two police officers in hot pursuit. As all three of them descended into the main foyer, they scattered mums and toddlers out of their way.

Casey heard Dom shout, 'Finlay! Wherever you are, get out of the damn way!'

But Finlay had other ideas. He knew about cops and bad men who broke the law. Mummy was a cop. But Mummy couldn't see him. She was looking in the wrong direction. So was Daddy. The other policemen weren't getting very far because everyone was getting in their way.

Chubbins would come to the rescue.

Chubbins always did. Lucky he was hiding right behind him. Here came the bad man now.

'Go, Chubbins!' Finlay shouted as, with one massive heave, he pushed the cardboard cat with all his might. An angry roar followed as the man came crashing to the ground and the two policemen fell on top of him.

Finlay laughed and clapped with delight as the naughty man finally gave up his struggle and submitted to the handcuffs, and he was swept up in Mummy's arms.

★ ★ ★

'Mr Cross, you've been charged with wilful obstruction of a police officer while in pursuit of his duty.' Casey smiled pleasantly at Fraser Cross, who slouched like a sullen schoolboy on the other side of the desk. He sat up very suddenly, roused by her words.

'Ouch, don't give me that! You've made that up and that solicitor will back me up as soon as he gets here. Where is he, by the way?' He pushed up his sleeve to check the time, before remembering his watch had been taken off him at the desk alongside the contents of his pockets.

'He'll be along shortly,' Casey reassured him.

'It was your officers doing the obstructing. Them and the wee boy who tried to knock me unconscious with a cardboard cat,' he continued. '*I* was simply exercising my right to go about my lawful business.'

Casey suppressed a smile. The 'wee boy' was now at home with his father, completely oblivious to the fact that he'd managed to achieve in moments what the Brockhaven Constabulary had failed to do in two days, i.e. finally get Fraser Cross in custody.

'Mr Cross, if you'd co-operated with my officers initially we could have got to the bottom of this by now,' Casey said. 'The fact that you failed to co-operate twice might suggest to some that you have a guilty conscience.'

'Mebbe. But then you're a copper. You possess a copper's lack of imagination.'

Casey stretched her lips in a humourless smile.

'Whereas to me and other honest citizens like me it's more likely to suggest that my actions were nothing more than a desperate act of self-preservation to avoid being fitted up.'

Casey struggled to remain civil. 'I assure you, Mr Cross, that I have never 'fitted anyone up', as you call it, for anything,' she said.

A sharp rap at the door announced the arrival of the duty solicitor. Casey recognised him immediately: Giles Woolley. Woolley the Weasel, as he was known behind his back, for reasons which were bound to manifest themselves during the course of the interview. Casey waited for him to take his seat.

'You've read the charge and Mr Cross's statement?'

'I have.' Giles Woolley sniffed the air as if seeking a way out of a trap. Casey decided to offer him one. 'Well, I'm dropping them,' she said. Turning to Fraser Cross, she added, 'I'm not interested in bringing charges against you for what happened earlier.'

Fraser Cross, initially taken aback by

her remark, made to get up once it had sunk in, but the solicitor motioned him to remain where he was, whereupon Cross fixed him with a hard stare. 'Whose side are you on, pal? She's said I can go, so I'm going.'

'Let's just hear what the inspector has to say, shall we?' The Weasel dismissed Cross's pugilistic stance with a shuffle of his papers.

'Look,' Casey sighed. 'I'm putting put my cards on the table. I have another agenda.'

★ ★ ★

Fraser Cross let out an exasperated sigh and slumped back down in his seat. 'I knew it,' he moaned.

'Morris Greenwood is dead. Amphetamines were found in his bloodstream. His — er — girlfriend, Flora Curtiss, insists he would never take anything which would react badly with the heart medication he took. She also said that two weeks ago, as she was climbing the stairs to Mr Greenwood's office back in

London, she heard you threaten him.'

'You what? What am I supposed to have said?' Fraser Cross searched her face for clues.

' "You'd better watch your back if you know what's good for you." ' Casey read out the words from Flora Curtiss's statement in a voice devoid of all emotion.

Fraser Cross gave a snort of contemptuous laughter.

'She also said that Mr Greenwood, previous to that threat, had informed you he could no longer represent you as an agent.'

'Well, she got that bit right,' he said. 'Thanks for reminding me. Just when I was getting over it, too.'

The Weasel began to paw the air. Casey deduced that a question had occurred to him. Quite an important one, as it turned out. '*Did* you say it, Mr Cross?' he huffed.

Fraser Cross, who appeared to be giving the question some consideration, stared at his hands. He might speak with the accent of a man desperately clinging to his roots, Casey mused, but his hands were those of an artist. Finally, he deigned to reply.

'I may have done. I've said a lot of things in my life. But I don't remember every word.'

Casey got the impression that deep down he was enjoying this. No doubt he'd store it up in his writer's brain, bring it out a couple of years down the line, give it a bit of a polish and slap it in a novel. Probably with herself cast in the role of a modern-day Lestrade, the idiot police inspector who was constantly bested by Sherlock Holmes. Which, even in her own eyes, was no more than she deserved, frankly. Though maybe she had McGovern to thank for casting in her in that role. It was at his insistence that this charade was taking place, after all. Her own private research had led her down a different path entirely.

'Come to think of it, aye. She's right. I did say that. I said a great deal more too, most of it unrepeatable. But I didn't kill the man, Inspector. Though at the time nothing would have given me greater pleasure than to slug him one in the face and lay him out.'

The Weasel rubbed his nose with his

paw and grimaced.

'You must know I've got form, right?' So, finally Cross had decided to put *his* cards on the table.

'I know you have a conviction for GBH,' she admitted.

The Weasel began twitching again.

'To my eternal shame,' Cross admitted. 'There was a woman involved. I loved her but she preferred someone else. I punched him. It was a long time ago. Call it the hot-headedness of youth.'

'That's not what the judge called it. He said it was a callous attack on a man in his own home.'

'Exactly! I punched him. In full view of my ex and a few others too, if I remember rightly. I think they were having a dinner party at the time.' He spread his hands pleadingly. 'Inspector, look at me. Do I look like the kind of guy who would try and get his revenge by slipping a few uppers into his intended victim's glass of wine?' His words were uncannily similar to what she'd said to McGovern earlier. 'If I'd wanted to kill Morris Greenwood,' he said, not waiting for her reply, 'I'd have done it the day he told me he'd decided to end our contract. Act first, think second — that's more my style, Inspector.'

Casey snapped shut the file that was open in front of her. Enough of this timewasting. She had people to see, places to go. 'Right, Mr Cross. I think that will be all for now. You're free to go.'

'I am?' He almost looked disappointed. No doubt she'd spoiled his research.

'Yes. No charges.'

The Weasel's bemused expression changed to one of relief as her words sank in and he shuffled to his feet. Easiest money he'd earned in a long while, Casey mused as she led them to the door.

'I'll accompany you off the premises,' she said. She desperately needed to stretch her legs.

At the desk, the duty officer proceeded to empty the contents of a small tray containing Fraser Cross's belongings onto the desk. 'Keys, wallet, pink purse, mobile phone, roll-up papers and tobacco,' he said, ticking them off his list.

'Oops! Now you're going to nick me again.' Cross picked up the pink suede purse and waved it in Casey's face. 'Strictly speaking this doesn't belong me,' he said. 'I saw someone drop it the other day.'

Casey was intrigued. This was ringing a loud bell. Earlier, waiting for her interview with Cross to start, she'd glanced through a report about the latest victims of the so-called Brockhaven Bag Snatcher — as the *Gazette* liked to call them in true innaccurate tabloid style. Hadn't she read there that someone had had a pink suede purse snatched?

She grabbed it from Fraser Cross's hand and opened it up. There was a name embossed in gold lettering in the pink silk lining. Fiona Stocks. That was definitely the same name she'd seen written in the report.

'You saw who dropped this, you said?'

'Like I said. I'd come out of the station and was standing with everyone else waiting for the little green man to tell me it was okay to cross the road. See, I don't always break the law, Inspector.' He looked pleased at his little joke. 'I saw it fall to the ground out of the corner of my eye. I was onto it in a flash. Picked it up and ran after her to return it, but she was too quick for me.'

'She? Can you describe her?'

Fraser Cross grinned uncharacteristically. 'I can do better than that,' he said. grabbing his phone and trawling through a menu. 'I'm always snapping people I see on the street. Nothing kinky, in case you've got me down for a pervert as well as a thief and a murderer. It's just something to do. My gallery of faces for when I need a face to match a character. Here.'

He held out the phone and Casey took it. The snap was head and shoulders only: a young, sullen-faced girl, with a stud in her nose and gelled up hair. Casey's heart missed enough beats to make her feel dizzy. She struggled to keep her voice steady.

'If you can just hang on a minute, Mr Cross, I need to upload this picture onto my computer,' she said, turning on her heel and heading for her office without bothering to wait for a reply.

★ ★ ★

Casey studied the face on her computer screen. There was no doubt about it. Less than two hours ago when she'd been in McGovern's office arguing about the unlikelihood of Fraser Cross having anything to do with Morris Greenwood's death, she'd stood face-to-face with the photograph on his desk: Mrs McGovern, his teenage daughter and his little boy.

This sullen-faced girl staring back at her on the screen was Kizzie McGovern — frozen in time, after believing herself to have got away with one of the oldest tricks in the book. Steal a purse, rifle through its contents, stash the cards and money and toss the evidence away. What good was an empty purse to anyone, anyway, was how their logic went.

Casey gnawed on a rough nail. So, what was she supposed to do now? Go marching into McGovern's office to inform him his daughter was a tea-leaf? Or pretend she hadn't seen the picture evidence and hope it would go away? She was no fan of McGovern's; she made no bones about it. But he was a colleague and he was a father too. As a colleague he would be humiliated when details of his daughter's deeds came to light — and come to light they would have to. And as a father . . . well, how did any parent square their child's behaviour when it reflected so badly back on them?

Casey continued to stare at the girl's face for a full minute, turning over the alternatives in her mind. Then she leaned forward and switched off the computer. She was going to need a night's sleep before she could touch this one.

* * *

Casey had arrived at Daisy Bannister's house alone and unnanounced. It was her second stop of the day. Pulling up outside the thatched cottage bathed in warm sunlight, she was reminded of a different world from the one she inhabited. One where people took tea at five o'clock and wrote letters and wore different clothes on Sundays.

Then she remembered the flipside to the idyll. She'd switched off enough episodes of *Midsomer Murders* and guessed the plots of enough Agatha Christie novels to know that not everything in the English country garden was rosy.

Casey couldn't help feeling disappointed when Daisy Bannister answered the door herself, instead of a genuflecting maid in a mob cap and apron. She was dressed in something pink that Casey imagined might have been called a leisure suit in the fashion pages circa 1987. She wore her glasses on a chain around her neck and was holding a gold pen. She looked more than slightly irritated at having being called away from her muse.

'I do hope I'm not interrupting anything.' Casey proffered her I.D. card. 'Only, I was there at your signing yesterday when that kerfuffle broke out.'

Daisy Bannister shifted her gaze from Casey's face to her I.D. card and back again. 'Well, actually,' she said, 'I'm just in the middle of something.'

'I'm sure. But I thought you'd want to know how the story ended. You being a writer and everything.' Casey slipped her I.D. card back into her bag and brought out the half-dozen or so Chubbins books

Daisy Bannister had failed to sign, thanks to Fraser Cross's uninvited guest appearance at her promotion event.

Daisy Bannister's hostess smile faltered but, albeit grudgingly, she relented, leading Casey inside, through the hallway and into a shabby conservatory. Hastily, she pushed a pile of papers aside and gestured for Casey to set the books down in the space on the table she'd created.

'Whose name shall I put?' She opened the first book — *Chubbins Wins The Race* — and waited for Casey's reply, pen poised. Casey supplied her with Finlay's name, obligingly spelling it.

'So. You've charged this Fraser Cross, then?' Daisy Bannister signed with a flourish.

'Cross? No. I'm afraid we found no evidence. Mr Cross has gone back to London as far as I know.'

A flicker of unease crossed Daisy Bannister's face.

'Perhaps you could put the date, too,' Casey prompted. 'Dates are really rather significant, don't you think?'

Daisy Bannister's plump fingers grasped

the pen as she scrawled the date, Finlay's name and her signature.

'Does the date 5 September, 1992 hold any significance for you, Mrs Bannister?' Casey bided her time before obliging Daisy Bannister with a prompt. 'It was a Saturday.'

The question hovered in the air between them for a long time. When it became apparent that Daisy Bannister wasn't interested in entering into a dialogue on this particular subject, Casey supplied the reply herself.

'Well, of course you do,' she said. 'Who could forget their wedding day?'

'Okay. So I was married to Morris,' Daisy Greenwood snapped. 'It was a long time ago.'

'And you never got divorced?'

She shook her head, refusing to say one way or the other. Again, Casey spoke for her. 'The marriage lasted two years. You never divorced because there was never any reason to. Until a few weeks ago when Morris wrote to you telling you he wanted to marry Flora Curtiss.'

The same Flora Curtiss who'd left a

message at the station late last night to say she didn't know if it was important, but she'd just remembered that she'd had a call from someone who said she was a journalist on the morning of Morris's death, asking if she'd be willing to meet for an interview. Only, when she'd arrived at the meeting point there was no journalist. When she came back Morris's mood was subtly different from how it had been before she left. 'Quieter, more subdued' had been her words. But back to the present.

'For years you made a good living and could well afford to keep yourself in the luxury to which you'd grown accustomed.' Casey cast her eyes around the shabby room. It may have been luxurious once upon a time. But now it was badly in need of renovation. 'Your investments were doing well too. For a time. But then you bought that land in Spain with a view to building your own property on it. A writer's retreat, wasn't it mean to be?'

Daisy Bannister glared at her. 'Who told you this?'

'Brockhaven's a small town, Ms

Bannister. The writing community is even smaller. It didn't take me long to find the right people to ask.'

Brockhaven Writers had been going for years. She'd gone straight to the chair, no less than Zoë Steel, organiser of the Lit Fest. What she didn't know about Daisy Bannister's disastrous business dealings just wasn't worth knowing.

'But then the Spanish government declared your lovely half-built writer's retreat was standing in the way of their motorway. And that was that. The compensation you received barely covered the cost of solicitors' fees. What to do now, eh? Especially when the worry of it all meant the ideas for the books stopped flowing and the royalties and advances began to dry up?'

Daisy Bannister groped for a chair and sat down in it heavily. She looked suddenly old and ill. Casey felt almost cruel as she went on to inform here what CCTV at the hotel had revealed this very morning: footage of Flora Curtiss leaving to meet her non-existent journalist and minutes later a beaming Daisy Bannister showing up at reception.

'He'd written me letters,' she said, suddenly defiant. 'I tore them up. When he called me, saying we needed to talk, I slammed the phone down on him. So when I turned up he wasn't expecting me. He thought I was going to say, fine, go ahead, congratulations. But I said if he thought I was going to step aside so easily he had another thing coming. That's when he went into one of his panics.' She pursed her lips disapprovingly. 'Morris was always far too highly strung,' she said.

'So what did you do then?'

'I gave him a couple of my pills. Course, he thought they were for dyspepsia. I take them occasionally when I have an idea and I want to stay up all night to follow it.' She eyed Casey coolly. 'The rest you know, I think. Are you going to read the charge now, Inspector?' she said.

* * *

Casey and Dom strolled along the pier, Finlay asleep in his pushchair.

'You must stop beating yourself up

59

about Lucy McGovern, Casey.'

'I know. You've said. It was only a matter of time before somebody caught her. It just so happened it was me and not some other copper.'

'Some other copper wouldn't have handled it as well as you.'

'Maybe.' Casey sighed. 'I just wish I could help McGovern more. He's a broken man, Dom, you know? And there's his wife and their other kid too. Not to mention Lucy herself. How screwed up must she be to get involved in theft?'

Thank God she was to be spared having to interview the girl. Casey had no idea how on earth she'd have been able to get through that ordeal.

'They'll get through it.' Dom put a comforting arm round Casey's shoulder. 'You can snap an individual in two just as easily as if he were a twig. But a family — well, a family is like a bundle of twigs. Tie them up tight together and there's no way that bundle can be snapped.'

Casey gave Dom a squeeze. 'That's a lovely thing to say, Dom.'

She had a question she longed to ask

him. Given his previous display of metaphor she decided that now was the right time.

'Dom,' she ventured. 'Are you writing a novel?'

He narrowed his eyes. 'Am I what? What makes you think that?'

Casey grew suddenly flustered and started fussing round Finlay, who'd just woken up and was demanding a drink. Was she losing her touch,she wondered?

'There's no money in novels these days,' he said. 'Now, if you'd said screenplay, you'd be nearer the mark.' He eyed her suspiciously. 'How did you guess?'

She could have put it down to a woman's intuition. But she preferred to say it was because she was a damned good detective. The signs were there and all she did was follow the trail, she confessed.

'Let me buy us all an ice cream,' she said. 'And I'll tell you how I worked it all out.'

Hide and Seek

1

Isobel sat Debs down with a cup of tea.

'You look like you need one,' she said. 'What on earth's the matter?'

Debs had worked as a cleaner and occasional childminder for Isobel, who was an English lecturer at the university, for over a year now. During this time, their relationship had evolved from one of employer and employee into one of friendship.

She accepted the tea readily, but when it came to explaining what the matter was she found she didn't know where to start. So many things about Tony's unexpected phone call had got to her that it was proving hard to separate her true concerns from the ancient grudge she'd held against him ever since he'd walked out on her for another woman, abandoning his daughter in the process.

Isobel was almost as shocked as Debs had been, when she heard that Tony

Randall was offering to take Chelsea skiing at half-term.

'But that's next week!' she cried. 'It's not much notice.'

'Well, yes, Isobel,' Debs agreed. 'But, actually, that's not the most surprising thing. There's the slight matter of him leaving it practically seven years before deciding he wanted to make contact with Chelsea again.'

'Of course,' Isobel said, suitably chastised. 'Why the sudden reawakened interest, you mean?'

'Tony's got a new wife now and a four-year-old daughter,' Debs reminded Isobel.

'Same age as my Abbie, then.'

Debs nodded. She didn't even know what Tony's daughter was called. She knew *her* name, though, the wife. Andrea.

'He's been out of our lives since Chelsea was seven. She's fifteen now, nearly, and apart from the first couple of years, when there was a card and the odd phone call, there's been nothing. And now this.'

'Have you mentioned it to Chelsea

yet?' Isobel asked.

Debs shook her head glumly. She didn't look forward to that, at all. Chelsea would bite her hand off. A skiing trip to Switzerland! How cool would that sound when she let it drop at school?

'The thing is, I've made a rod for my own back by never saying one harsh word about Tony to Chelsea. As far as she's concerned, he's sweetness and light. I can hardly turn round now and tell her I don't want her to go because I think he'll probably let her down again, can I?'

Isobel wrinkled her brow and gazed into the distance. Debs recognised that look. She was about to apply her fierce intellect to the problem. And Debs guessed it would come down in Tony's favour, because in Isobel's world, intellect beat emotion every time.

Until it came to Robby, her latest boyfriend, that is. Or toyboy, as Debs couldn't help thinking of him. What else would you call someone twelve years Isobel's junior — one of her PhD students, too! Ex-public school, superior kind in Debs' mind — charming to a fault. She trusted Robby even less than she trusted Tony.

'You know, Debs, this might be just the opportunity for you to start taking back some time for yourself,' Isobel said, breaking through her thoughts. 'You've raised Chelsea single-handedly all these years, after all.'

'And I've loved it.' Debs was beginning to feel she needed to justify herself.

'You've done a splendid job, too,' Isobel said diplomatically. 'Only sometimes you can love too much.'

'You think I'm over-protective, don't you?'

'No! Not at all!' she protested. 'It's just — I know how grateful I am that Oliver has never quibbled about sharing the childcare. It's meant I've been able to hold on to the me I was before Abbie came along. And not having her around some evenings and weekends means Robby can sometimes stay over, of course.'

Isobel got this soppy, loved-up look on her face whenever Robby's name was mentioned. Fine if you were a teenager, but Isobel was her own age, give or take a couple of years. Well, five or six, maybe. Debs eased herself out of her chair.

'I'd better get on,' she said, making her way to the door.

'Just think about it, Debs. That's all I'm saying,' Isobel said to her retreating back.

Thinking about it was exactly what Debs managed to avoid doing as she went about her routine. Robby had been there the previous night, she noticed, as her eyes swept over the toiletries on the bathroom shelf. He used more grooming products than she did! Picking up a random jar, she unscrewed a lid and sniffed it. In her day, men didn't wear moisturiser.

She caught a glance of her reflection and the unflattering expression of disapproval on it. Not to mention the nest of crows' feet jostling for space around her eyes. And was that another grey hair?

'You're becoming a grumpy old woman, Debs,' she said, shaking her head sadly. 'Isobel's right. You need to get out more.'

She stuck her head round Isobel's bedroom door. Robby had left a pile of his clothes in the middle of the floor.

Debs gave the rumpled shirt and trousers and disapproving shake then folded them neatly. As she went to lay them over the back of a chair, something fell out of one of the pockets, onto the floor.

Debs bent to retrieve it and was in the middle of scrutinising the contents of a small, self-seal clear plastic bag, when Isobel, dressed in her coat ready to leave for the college department, wandered into the room, startling her.

'Debs, before I go I need to remind you the odd-job man's coming to see to that dripping tap so will you . . . '

She stopped short, her eyes drawn to Debs' frozen stance and the packet she held in her hands.

'I — it dropped out of Robby's pocket,' Debs said nervously. 'What do you think it is it?'

She'd watched enough TV to be familiar with what cocaine looked like, but still she kept on hoping it was simply a bag of sugar, or something equally innocuous.

'I'll kill him!' Isobel snatched the bag from Debs' hand. 'Bringing that stuff into my house and with Abbie around, too.

What on earth is he thinking about?'

Debs had never seen Isobel so furious before.

'Just wait till I get my hands on him!'

Debs looked on, amazed, as Isobel scattered the contents of the bag on to the floor, seized the vacuum cleaner and, her face grim with purpose, sucked up every single trace of the white powder. It was almost funny, Debs thought, but maybe she was the only one who thought so.

'Right,' Isobel said. 'I'm off to find him. We've got some serious talking to do.'

It was as if a whirlwind had swept through the house, Debs thought, as the front door slammed so hard behind her that the house shook to its foundations. She couldn't help admiring Isobel for showing no signs of being fearful of a confrontation. On the contrary, she looked like she was looking forward to it.

Debs didn't fancy being Robby when Isobel got hold of him, not that he deserved sympathy.

A knock on the door made her jump. What if it were Robby, who, having realised what he'd left behind, had returned to retrieve it before Isobel found it With a quaking heart, she opened the door, her face already prepared in an expression that said she knew nothing about anything.

'Mrs Murray? You reported a dripping tap.'

The man at the door flashed his card. *Jim Collier*, it said, *handyman. All household tasks undertaken.* Underneath his name was a mobile number and e-mail address. It took a moment for Debs to remember Isobel's only half-delivered message.

'Of course,' she said. 'The kitchen's this way.'

She led him through, wondering whether to offer him a cup of tea, or not. But if the job only took a minute, then she'd be forced to stand there making small talk while he waited for his tea to become cool enough to drink, and she had so much more to do before she picked little Abbie up from nursery.

'A new washer, Mrs Murray,' he declared, after a quick inspection of the offending tap. 'Won't take a minute.'

'That's relief,' she said. 'I've had

enough excitement for one morning.'

'Like that, is it?'

'The trouble with me,' Debs thought, 'is that I can't bear to keep my distance from strangers. The first sign of interest from a fellow human being and I'm off.' Hadn't she just sworn not to engage in chit-chat? Now, here she was, on the verge of offering up her day's woes — or a highly edited version of them, at least — to this, admittedly, sympathetic-looking man.

'Oh, you know,' she hedged. 'Too much to do and too little time to do it in.'

'You just get on then, Mrs Murray,' he said, deftly unscrewing the tap. 'I'll be out of your hair in no time.'

Nice chap, Debs thought, half an hour later, after they'd exchanged goodbyes and she was on her way out to the nursery. Maybe she should have put him straight about her identity, though. But what could it possibly matter to either of them in the end if he'd confused the cleaning lady with the owner of the house? He'd got his money and she'd probably never see him again. 'Honestly, sometimes, Debs,' she told herself as she rang the buzzer to be admitted into the nursery, 'If you didn't have enough to worry about then you'd start looking for it.'

★   ★   ★

A week had passed since Tony's first phone call and what had begun as his tentative and, predictably from Tony's point of view, generous, offer had become a reality. Just as she'd expected, Chelsea had almost bitten off her hand in her enthusiasm for the idea. What followed was a flurry of list-making, shopping and phone calls to settle the arrangements.

And now, at a quarter to four in the morning, Chelsea was gone. Less than a minute ago, Tony's car had driven away from the front of the house with a buoyant Chelsea, plus far too much luggage on board. Discreetly, Debs had positioned herself at her bedroom window, anxiously peering out on to the perfor-mance below — Chelsea dancing round the car and chattering nineteen to the dozen while a much fatter Tony than she remembered attempted a number of solutions to storing Chelsea's bags, before finally arriving at the most satisfactory.

She knew it had been cowardly of her not to go downstairs and at least acknowledge Tony face to face. But she'd said all she needed to say about her expectations of him regarding Chelsea's welfare while she was in his care in one brief phone conversation. Fortunately, Chelsea was so excited about leaving that she hadn't even noticed Debs' reluctance to come downstairs and wave her off.

She should go back to bed, she told herself, but, reluctant to leave until she could no longer hear Tony's engine, she remained where she was. The street was deserted apart from the neighbour's cat, sniffing the pavement diffidently as he ambled along.

Of course, she'd had the thought before, but now it hit her fully. The longest she and Chelsea had ever been apart was for a night at a time, when Chelsea had been invited to sleepovers by friends. Debs was going to miss her terribly. The lump in her throat and the prickle of tears she'd been fighting to keep out snuck in anyway, as she'd known they would even before she kissed Chelsea goodbye.

'Come on, Debs,' she said aloud. 'It's not all bad.'

Determinedly, she turned her mind to the one thing that had buoyed her up all last week, when hearing Tony's voice after such a long absence stirred up all those bad memories. She had good old Mr Rutherford, or Ed, as he insisted on being called, to thank for that. Ed was her Friday person and during the hours of nine and midday on that day each week Debs would be there, cleaning his house.

Last Friday had started the same as any other, with a cup of tea and a catch-up, which always involved Ed giving forth on his favourite subject of how England was going to the dogs. Too many people with degrees in media studies, according to Ed, and not enough who could fix things when they broke. It had been at that exact moment that the doorbell rang.

'Thank the Lord for you, Jim, that's all I can say,' he'd cried, flinging open the door dramatically — Ed had, once upon a time, been the leading light of the local am-dram society and still had a tendency to play to the gallery.

Framed in the doorway was the man who'd come to fix Isobel's dripping tap, earlier in the week. Debs recognised him at once. Maybe, unconsciously, she'd been thinking of him on and off ever since — his solid presence and thoughtful, steady gaze, like he was weighing up what was wrong and how soon he could fix it even as he walked into the house.

This morning he'd come to have a look at Edward's back door, which had swollen in the rain and become difficult to shut. It meant a longer visit than the one he'd paid to Isobel's, involving several cups of tea.

'You get around,' she'd said jokily, emboldened by the fact that Ed was at her shoulder.

He'd replied how he'd been thinking exactly the same himself. There followed a long unravelling of how she came to be living in two different houses, which she wasn't, of course. No, she wasn't Mrs

Murray, even though she'd answered Mrs Murray's door. Her name was Debs Randall. And Ed Rutherford wasn't her father either, but someone else for whom she worked. The ice well and truly broken, for the rest of the morning, each time she popped into the kitchen for something, Jim would look up from his task and nod a greeting.

Jim would be paying a second visit to Edward's next Friday, to have a look at his guttering, Debs remembered. He'd wanted to return immediately after the weekend, but Ed wouldn't hear of it. He had too many other commitments, he insisted. So, Friday it would have to be then, Jim had said.

She smiled to herself when she remembered looking at Ed's calendar on the kitchen notice board just before she left the house. He was a stickler for writing down all his appointments. *When you get to my age, Debs, you can't risk relying on your short-term memory*, he'd said, on more than one occasion.

Odd then, that there'd been nothing pencilled in at all for the upcoming week.

When she'd questioned this, after Jim had left, Ed had readily owned up to doing a bit of matchmaking. *You're a fine-looking woman, Debs,* he'd said, making her blush to the roots of her hair. *And if I'm not mistaken, Jim's just as smitten as you are.* Of course, she'd laughed it off, but the prospect of seeing Jim again soon had stopped her from dwelling on Chelsea's imminent absence.

Something else to be cheerful about was the prospect of Abbie coming to stay tomorrow, too — although she had to admit it had taken her aback when Isobel informed her she was taking Robby to Madrid with her as her plus one. Debs had known for months all about the academic conference Isobel was to attend in Spain, where she was to give a paper. She'd been really looking forward to it. Oliver, Isobel's ex, had agreed to have Abbie and Isobel was excited that she'd get time to explore without having to rush back as soon as the conference was over.

But after her display of fury when she'd discovered the cocaine, Debs had been certain that Isobel would finish with Robby. They'd made it up, was all Isobel would divulge, when Debs had shown her surprise. There'd be no more drugs, end of story, she'd said, and Debs, quickly sensing Isobel didn't want to go into details, backed off. Robby had used his persuasive charms on her, obviously, and she'd fallen for it, hook, line and sinker.

But the day after Isobel sprang this announcement on her, she'd rung Debs to say that Oliver had let her down at the last minute — something to do with his mother being rushed into hospital — and could Debs have Abbie? Debs found herself agreeing, with the stipulation that it was at her house.

Abbie was a lovely child and she'd be company, even up in Chelsea's room asleep while she was downstairs, whiling away the evening watching TV.

As she was about to close the curtains, with the intention of going back to bed and snatching a few more hours, a dark-coloured van turned into the road and drew up outside Isobel's. Then Robby got out. She couldn't see his face in the dark, but from his slumped shoulders and his slow, weary walk to Isobel's door, he looked rather dejected. What a time to be coming in, Debs mused. Just as many people were thinking of getting up.

⋆ ⋆ ⋆

He was in big trouble. But he had to do it. It wasn't like he had a choice. Not when he owed all that money. How had Fynn let it creep up to that amount without demanding that Robby paid up? Because making money from gullible people was his business, that's why, and he'd seen Robby coming.

Just a bit of blow for the weekend, Rob? Can't pay me right now? No worries. I know you're good for it.

And like a fool Robby had thought Fynn meant it. That it *was* possible to be mates with your dealer. He should have known all the backslapping and the repeated reassurances that Robby could pay him whenever he felt like it would be thrown back in his face sooner or later.

Now, later had finally arrived. And unless he did what Fynn wanted, he was finished.

'Come on, Robby, think,' he urged himself, gazing down at the innocuous-looking supermarket carrier bag on his lap. 'You've got to find a hiding place for this weapon until Fynn needs it.' No use asking him again how long he thought that might be. He'd already tried it. *You're in no position to be asking questions*, had been Fynn's reply, delivered with that sly smile of his which Robby, scales finally fallen from his eyes, realised he'd been misinterpreting for far too long.

He couldn't hide it in his flat. There was no lock on the door of his room, for one thing, and the other postgrads he shared with hadn't really learned the meaning of the word *private*. But if Isobel found out that he was a) holding a gun and b) holding it because he'd defaulted on his payment for all the cocaine he'd had off Fynn, she'd go crazy.

Especially after he'd promised her, practically on bended knees, that after that wrap the cleaner had found there'd be no more drug-taking. He could have lied, said it wasn't his. But Isobel had been terrifying. Going on and on about Abbie, and what could have happened if she'd discovered it. He'd have agreed to anything just to shut her up.

And then he had a brainwave. Abbie. Yes. Of course. If you waited long enough there'd always be an answer. Leaping nimbly from his seat, Robby crept up the stairs and pushed open the door to Abbie's room.

At the foot of her bed stood her chest of toys. Inside, he knew, was her stash of dolls and teddies. No need to creep when he went to lift the lid either, which was sweet, because, just like her mother, nothing woke her but the need for food.

Riffling through the contents, Robby rejected a rag doll and several smaller teddies for one he thought would be just dandy. A monstrous great pink shaggy thing. The perfect hiding place.

★ ★ ★

Isobel was getting into a panic. If she didn't calm down Abbie would pick up her tension. Then it would be up to Debs to sort it out once Isobel and Robby were in their taxi on their way to the airport. If Robby ever turned up, that was.

'I'm sure he'll be here any minute,' she said, keeping her tone upbeat. 'His last message said there was absolutely no need for you to worry.'

Isobel, her mobile clamped to her hand like a third limb, obviously didn't share Debs' confidence. Her mood was catching, Debs decided. She couldn't wait for Robby and Isobel to be in that taxi on their way to the airport so that she and Abbie could just chill out and have some fun.

'Did you bring any board games?' she asked, determined to change the focus away from Robby's tardiness.

Isobel, miles away, said she couldn't remember, which gave Debs the perfect opportunity to offer to pop across to look for some.

'I can be back in a second, so text me when the taxi gets here,' she said, making a break for it.

This trip is doomed, she thought, as she let herself inside Isobel's house. What if being late is Robby's way of telling her that he really can't be bothered with this Spanish trip and Isobel can't see it?

Oh, well, better assume he *will* be here before the airport taxi is, she told herself, sprinting up the stairs and into Abbie's room.

'For goodness' sake, Isobel!' she cried out, once inside. It was clear that all Isobel had been able to focus on was her own trip. It had certainly occurred to Debs that the case she'd brought for Abbie was small, but even so, she'd assumed she'd at least included some toys and books.

But here were two of Abbie's favourite jigsaws, some of the pieces still scattered around the floor from the last time she'd used it. And there was her precious alphabet floor puzzle that she'd got so excited about finally getting the hang of.

With a sigh of exasperation, Debs gathered up all the pieces of the various puzzles and crammed them back into their boxes. Then, needing something to carry them back over the road in, she nipped next door to the spare room, to see if she could find something suitable.

Grabbing a discarded laundry bag, Debs dropped everything inside. Even if it only had one handle, it would do. And then Debs' eyes alighted on a large, rather hairy and very pink teddy sitting on the highest shelf and she laughed aloud. She wouldn't have been at all surprised if someone had bought this for Abbie, and Isobel, taking against its brashness, had simply hidden it away in a room Abbie never entered.

'What harm could it possibly do the child?' she thought. Without further ado, she grabbed it, and headed down the stairs with the rest of her booty. As she opened the front door, she heard the unmistakeable sound of a taxi chugging down the street, and there was Isobel at Debs' front door signalling for her to get a move on.

'I'm there already,' she yelled, as she struggled across the street, her bag of toys in one hand and the teddy, even more nauseatingly pink in daylight, in the other.

2

The first time Isobel met Robby socially, she was wearing the proverbial beer goggles. It had been a celebration of sorts, if you could so describe the end of a marriage that imploded almost as soon as the ink was dry on the marriage certificate. But a couple of her oldest girlfriends had insisted she absolutely must not be allowed to sit at home moping over Oliver, and since she'd already booked Debs' daughter to babysit, she couldn't really wriggle out of it.

She'd been attempting to order another round of drinks at the bar, but the girl serving kept on ignoring her for whichever man caught her eye. Isobel was getting crosser and crosser, and wondering what on earth had happened to the sisterhood, when Robby stepped in and saved the day.

At first, she was just grateful he'd spotted the unfairness of the system.

'It could have turned ugly back then,' she said with a grin, once the drinks were in front of them.

'You look like you could handle yourself,' he said, brushing her hand as he passed her the beer she'd ordered. His eyes flickered over her face and body in the way that men had been programmed to follow ever since Adam first spotted Eve weaving a daisy chain in the Garden of Eden. Fifteen years ago, at Chelsea's age, she'd have loathed it. But tonight she was flattered to think this tall, lean youth with hair like bath bubbles and a jaw like a Greek god thought that this older woman was worth expending a bit of patter on. It was at that exact moment she knew she wanted him.

Nothing happened that night — she was with her friends and Robby appeared to be with his. But for the rest of the evening she was distracted, unable to get him out of her head, pretending she wasn't checking him out when she was, and suddenly losing interest in being there at all, once she realised that he'd left.

She hadn't had beer goggles on the following day, though, when Robby had knocked on her door for his tutorial. His supervisor, Dr Thomas, had been taken ill, he said. She must know about it, it was the talk of the department. She did know, of course. A brain tumour, such a terrible thing. So sad, a family man, brilliant career ahead of him, too. All this while she ran her eye over the list of student names. And there was Robby's. Fate had allocated him to her list, and, less than a week later, he was in her bed.

Isobel hovered by the window, taut with nerves, praying for Robby to turn the corner. Any minute now the taxi would be here to pick them up to take them to the airport. What on earth was keeping him? At this rate, Debs would be back before him.

She knew Debs thought she was making a big mistake giving Robby a second chance. But then Debs had disapproved of Robby from day one. Not that she ever expressed it verbally. That wasn't Debs' way. Isobel didn't believe she'd ever heard Debs speak ill of anyone

89

— not even that dodgy-sounding ex-husband of hers who'd turned up out of the blue offering to whisk Chelsea away on a skiing trip with him and his new family.

But it was precisely Debs' silence on the subject of Robby that screamed loudest. She did her best to ignore it, of course. Debs was just narrow-minded in her opinion of who was suitable and who wasn't, that was all. Oliver had been suitable, hadn't he? Same age, same solid, middle-class background. And look where that had ended.

So what did it matter if Rob was twelve years her junior, and a bit of a toff? It wasn't as if she was looking for another husband, Good Lord, no. Right now, all she wanted was a good time, and Robby was excellent at providing her with that.

Except he hadn't quite been doing that recently. Today wasn't the first time he'd kept her waiting, and recently, even when he'd finally turned up, he'd been distant. She'd tried to draw him out, to find out what was on his mind, but he always brushed aside her concern. His moods never lasted long, fortunately. Half an hour later, he'd be waltzing her round the room, chattering nonsense, or carrying her up to bed for the kind of mind-blowing sex she'd only ever imagined when she'd been married to Oliver.

It was the sex that was the trouble, of course. She was an expert in English literature and had read enough books to know that it was always sex that was the trouble. If being in bed with Robby had been as tedious as it had quickly grown to be with Oliver, would she have forgiven him so readily for leaving that cocaine lying around? Somehow she doubted it. But not only had she forgiven him, she'd invited him to Madrid — provided he promised he'd never bring drugs into her house again. Now she had his word — but how reliable Robby's word proved to be, she was already beginning to doubt. After all, he'd promised he'd be here spot on the hour, and there was still no sign of him.

Here was Debs though, struggling to close Isobel's front door. What on earth was she carrying? She'd told Isobel she was just going to pick up a few board games for Abbie. But from the look of this, she'd ransacked the entire house! Oh, God, and now here was the taxi turning the corner. And then her phone bleeped a message.

Will meet you at check-in. Got delayed.

★ ★ ★

Debs knew something was up as soon as she saw Isobel's face.

'Change of plan,' she said, through clamped lips. 'I'm meeting Robby at the airport. So I'd better be getting on.' Then, casting a belligerent eye over Debs' trophies, she added 'What on earth have you dragged that thing over for? It's an eyesore.'

'The bear?' Debs took no offence at Isobel's sharp tone, under the circumstances. 'I thought he looked rather jolly, myself. A bit lonely sitting on the shelf, maybe. So I brought him along for some company.'

'You needn't have bothered. Abbie won't play with it — she's scared of the thing. Too big and ugly, which is exactly what I told Oliver when he threatened to buy it for her. Not that he took any notice, of course.'

Debs stood there, dangling the teddy from her arm, foolishly. 'I'm sorry,' she said.

There was a beat before Isobel, probably realising how harsh she must have sounded, returned one of her own.

'Nerves,' she said. 'Leaving Abbie for the first time. Flying. You know.'

'Abbie will be fine,' Debs said. 'She wouldn't settle for an afternoon nap so easily in a strange bed if she wasn't happy, would she? And the flight will be over before you know it.'

'Which only leaves Robby to worry about.' She didn't say, though it hung in the air like a bad smell.

'You're right,' Isobel mumbled, picking up her case. 'I'd better be off.' She waggled the pink teddy's lolloping arm, as she edged past Debs on her way out. 'Bye, both,' she added, in an attempt to alleviate the mood. 'Kiss Abbie for me.'

Debs grinned. 'I will. And have a good time,' she said.

At the door, Isobel turned round. She looked puzzled.

'Where did you say you found that great monstrosity, Debs?' she asked.

'The teddy? In the spare room. Top shelf. Why?'

'It's just that I thought I'd shoved it in the toy box. My mistake.'

And suddenly she was gone, leaving Debs cock-a-hoop with relief. She had her house to herself again, and never had her own space seemed so precious.

'Right, Ted,' she said, 'let's stick you some place where you won't frighten the horses before Abbie wakes up and takes it into her head to wander downstairs.'

The next day and a half was blissfully uneventful. Abbie seemed untroubled by Isobel's absence, which was hardly surprising, since Debs made a point of keeping to the little girl's routine as much as possible.

While Abbie was at nursery, Debs took advantage of the time she had for herself by getting her hair cut into a much younger, fresher style and having highlights added. She even managed a quick trip to a dress shop, where she picked up a new top in a flattering peach colour and a lipstick to match. She might only be cleaning Ed's kitchen sink in them, but she wasn't going to risk being caught in her oldest clothes by Isobel's odd-job man, Jim Collier, for the third time.

The hours when Abbie was awake were filled with the usual activities — games, walks, stories, baking. And there was the rub, she found herself thinking, as, the following afternoon, they trailed home from the playground at a snail's pace, Abbie's warm little hand in hers. Instead of taking her mind off her daughter's absence, spending so much time with Abbie was having quite the opposite effect.

Everything she'd done with Abbie this past day and a half she'd also done with Chelsea. Bathed her, made silly faces with peas and carrots to make sure she'd eat her vegetables, told her stories about her own childhood, on and on and more and more. And slap bang in the middle of whatever they'd been doing, Chelsea's face had suddenly risen up unbidden in her mind, and she'd found herself longing for her daughter's return.

She could ring her, of course. But she'd told Chelsea to go off and have a great time and only to ring if she was desperate. How would it seem to Chelsea, her mum calling her up every five minutes to ask her how she was? Needy, that was how it would sound. Pathetic, like she had no life of her own.

'Home at last!'

This was Abbie's latest phrase. She took such pleasure in language already, Debs noticed, beaming down at her as she scrabbled for her keys, in a hurry to get inside. They'd passed that beat-up, old, blue car again today, parked just a few doors up — she thought it was the same one that had dropped Robby off at Isobel's when she'd been seeing Chelsea off. No matter how much she fought it, its presence made her feel uneasy.

She hadn't heard footsteps approaching, so when she felt the hand on her shoulder she froze, though not before she'd taken Abbie by the shoulders and pushed her inside where she'd be safe.

'What do you want?' She spun round

and delivered her question in a strong voice that belied the shakiness she felt inside.

'I ain't meaning to scare you, lady, but I'm looking for someone and I'm wondering if you know where he is.'

The man was stocky. He could have been a boxer, Debs thought. His face was half-covered by the brim of a baseball cap and he was wearing the usual street garb of trainers, hoody and sweatpants. When he smiled it was with his mouth, but not his eyes.

'Who is it you're after?' Her voice was steady, but inside she was quaking with fear. A quick glance up and down the street revealed it to be deserted but for the two of them.

'Name of Rob. I gave him a lift down here one time, like. Only I forgot the house number.'

He smiled his bogus smile again. She knew no one of that name, she said, and, when the man went on to describe Robby, she insisted even more adamantly that no one of that description lived hereabouts, as far as she knew. Though that wasn't to say he mightn't, since she didn't know everyone.

The relief she felt when he was safely back in his car and driving off was palpable. She wondered what Robby had done to incur this visit, and, for a moment, it crossed her mind to ring Isobel to get her to warn him to watch his back. But what would be the point of spoiling Isobel's trip? There was nothing she could do about it. This was between Robby and his seeker.

★ ★ ★

'How could you?'

Isobel stood over Robby, glaring down at him. He sat hunched on the hotel bed, looking like a small boy accused of raiding the sweetie jar.

'I don't know, Isobel. They were there, and I was desperate.'

Isobel's diamond earrings, the only thing she'd inherited from her mother, were now back safely in their little velvet box, tucked away in her suitcase. Half an hour earlier, she'd walked in on Robby at the exact moment he was examining them in the palm of his hand. Wondering how much cocaine he could swap them for, no doubt. Or maybe giving himself time to work out how to say, 'Excuse me, but I wonder if you could direct me to the nearest crack den, please,' in Spanish.

'You promised me it was a one-off and that you were done with drugs!' she said.

'It was,' Robby replied. 'And I am.'

'Then why are you stealing from me?'

Robby buried his head in his hands.

'I'm sorry,' he mumbled. 'It was stupid. I was just bored. You'd be out at your conference all day and all I had to look forward to was being alone.'

He peered up at her through his fingers. He looked so helpless. But she wouldn't weaken. Not this time.

'No, Robby. I'm not having that. You've got the whole of Madrid to explore. Guided tour. Lunch all paid for while me and the rest of the delegates make do with a sandwich. If you'd rather do a couple of lines of coke than experience everything this city has to offer, then believe me, you've got a problem, even if you can't see it.'

Robby exhaled loudly but said nothing.

'You can get help for this,' she said.

'I don't need help,' Robby said. 'I'm not an addict.'

Isobel's patience had run out. She should be on her way to the lecture hall, right now. She'd only run back to change her jacket because she'd split juice on it at breakfast.

'Fine,' she snapped. 'But you are a thief.'

Robby's head shot up and he stared at her wide-eyed.

'Or do you deny that, too?' she said.

Robby shrugged. If he'd added 'whatever' she wouldn't have been at all surprised.

'It's over, Robby. I don't need you in my life.'

The words were out before she'd even formed them in her head. It was as if the scales had fallen from her eyes and she saw her affair with Robby for what it was. For him — convenience, a place to crash, someone to cook his meals and do his washing. And for her — well, she'd been flattered by a younger man's attentions.

So flattered she'd chosen to ignore the signs of addiction. His mood swings she'd put down to the vagaries of youth, because it was more convenient to think like that. But deep down she'd known that not even teenage boys could change their moods so suddenly from comatose to crazy.

'If you ask at reception, I'm sure they'll sort you out a plane,' she said, removing her other jacket from a hanger in the wardrobe. 'You'll be back at your place by nightfall.'

She watched him as her words sunk in. At your place, she'd said. Robby swallowed hard. Yes, he'd got the message. Tears welled up in her eyes as she pushed open the door and headed for the lift.

★ ★ ★

Chelsea wished she'd never come to Switzerland. She missed home and her mum so much. She'd looked forward to getting to know her dad again and had really tried to find out all about him and make a connection. But they just didn't seem to have even one thing in common.

She should have recognised it as an omen as soon as she got in the car. He'd stocked up on CDs for the car ride — top one hundred, bang up-to-the-minute stuff, he said. She liked classical music, and that old stuff from the 1980s Mum played. She belonged to the school orchestra and sang in the choir, so Girls Aloud didn't exactly float her boat, she told him when he asked what she thought of one particularly nauseating tune. He'd laughed at that, called her a funny little thing.

Andrea thought she was a funny little thing, too. Just because she didn't ogle the boys on the ski slope, or use make-up, or spend ages deciding what to put on every morning. They regarded her as a freak, obviously, because she didn't have Peaches Geldof as a role model and didn't want to be a pop star when she grew up.

From the kitchen, Andrea's cackle started up again. How could Dad ever have left Mum for someone so self-obsessed? All she talked about was celebrities and make-up and how many calories were contained in every single thing she put in her mouth.

Then there was Precious Molly. One stamp of her dainty little foot and everyone came running. Except that it had quickly become apparent to Chelsea that running after Molly on this particular holiday was the task that had been allocated to her. And that, apart from a session in the morning down the nursery slopes, was pretty much all she was here for.

Someone had to be there to escort Molly back to the chalet for a nap after lunch, while Andrea and Dad stayed in the bar and swapped skiing stories with their new best friends. And she couldn't possibly be left alone after dinner either, which is where Chelsea came in once more.

'You've got a real way with her,' Andrea had said, the first night they'd come back from the hotel bar, both the worse for drink. 'Nice and sisterly.'

The last thing Chelsea felt about Molly was sisterly, but she'd held her tongue. Nothing was said, but enough was implied. She was meant to be grateful.

For the trip, the new clothes, the opportunity to ski — such as it was — and, she got the feeling, for the privilege of being allowed to breathe the same air as Precious Molly.

Andrea came swaying out of the kitchen. She was like the percussion section in the orchestra. Ice cubes clinking on her wrist, earrings swishing backwards and forwards like windscreen wipers. Everything about her made a noise.

'Coo-ee, Chelsea! Nose in a book again? Molly's asking for you! Wants you to read her a story, bless!'

Chelsea forced a smile and slid noiselessly off the settee, before padding across the room on silent feet. 'It can be done, Andrea,' she felt like saying aloud, but she said it in her head instead.

'What's it to be, Molly? *Fancy Nancy* or *The Flower Princess*?'

⋆ ⋆ ⋆

'How come it's not where I put it? Oh, no! I could have sworn . . . I remember, clear as daylight, looking behind me to make sure Abbie was still sleeping, lifting the lid of her toy box. But I didn't put it back in there once I'd finished with it. I'm not that stupid, whatever Isobel thinks of me. I definitely brought it in here and put it up on the top shelf. So where is it?'

Robby sank to the ground, his back to the wall, and put his head in his hands. He felt a ringing in his ears and was sweating. The feeling of nausea that had begun the first time he'd opened the door of the spare room and failed to see the pink bear on the shelf where he'd left it was starting to overpower him.

Squatting on his haunches on the floor, he let rip with every swear word he knew. This teddy — or what it contained — was his means of getting himself off the hook. His lifesaver. How was he going to explain this to Fynn? The fact was, he couldn't. He was a dead man. Simple as that.

* * *

What had made Debs think of ringing Jim instead of the police when she saw the

105

light in Isobel's spare room flicker on and off, she didn't know. She peeped through her bedroom curtains, mug of hot milk in one hand, phone in the other, and waited nervously.

'I'll be there, pronto,' he'd said, just like he was used to being rung at three in the morning by damsels in distress. Not that she was much of a damsel, though she was certainly distressed by the thought of someone going through the contents of Isobel's house right before her eyes. And to think that she'd have missed it if little Abbie hadn't woken up, crying for her mummy for the first time since Isobel had been away.

At that moment, Jim's van turned into the road. And at the exact same moment the front door to Isobel's house opened to reveal a figure of someone she recognised. Robby! Wasn't he supposed to be in Madrid? What on earth was he doing skulking round Isobel's property at this time of the night? Well, thank God it wasn't a burglar. She could call off the hunt at least.

Only it was far too late to do that now.

Struck dumb by the speed at which it happened, all she could do was look on, aghast, as Jim, who'd clearly spotted Robby as soon as he'd let himself out of the house, leaped out of his van and hurled himself at Robby's legs, throwing the lighter man to the ground in an expert rugby tackle.

3

The silence in Debs' kitchen was as awkward as a rugby players pirouette. She was seriously regretting insisting Robby came over to her house to be checked out, after Jim's flying tackle. He'd made it plain he'd rather be anywhere but here.

She'd tried making small talk, but neither Robby nor Jim seemed inclined to join in. So, for twenty minutes, while she bustled about the kitchen, turning on the lights and heating, putting the kettle on and making tea, Robby simply sat hunched in his chair, staring at the floor. Every now and then he gave an occasional nervous sidelong glance at Jim, as if he expected him to take another swipe and wanted to be ready for it this time.

All she'd got out of him so far was that he'd decided to come back early from Madrid after a disagreement with Isobel and that he was on her property quite legitimately to collect some of his stuff.

She got even less from Jim after his initial gruff apology, when Debs had pelted outside to drag him off the poor lad. He seemed to have withdrawn completely from the situation. Something was going on inside his head, that much was obvious but, whatever it was, he was keeping it to himself for now.

It was a relief when she finally closed the door behind Robby.

'I'd best change your neighbour's locks first thing,' Jim said, on her return.

Debs gave a start at the sound of Jim's voice, after such a long silence.

'Isobel will be home tomorrow,' she said. 'You should talk to her first.'

'Just so she knows I'm happy to do the job,' he said. 'And the sooner the better, if you ask me.'

He drained the last of his tea and stood up to go. Debs felt a twinge of disappointment. Funny, but now Robby had left and they were alone, she was suddenly wide awake.

'You don't think he'll come back, do you?'

Her question was a delaying tactic.

'Just think about it, Debs,' he said, shrugging on his jacket. 'If he was going round there to pick up his stuff, then why did he come out of the house empty-handed?'

Debs admitted that was weird. 'I'll ring her in the morning,' she said, as she saw him to the door.

'Good. And don't forget to let me know when you've done it. I can be round in a jiffy.'

'Yes,' Debs said with a grin. 'I've seen how fast you can move.'

'Not bad when you consider the lad's barely in his twenties!'

Daylight was just breaking as the two of them stood in the open doorway, grinning at each other. Jim's kiss, when it came, was awkward and unexpected, but all the more welcome for that, in Debs' mind. The last man she'd kissed had been Tony, and she was out of practice. It was comforting to know that Jim was out of practice, too.

'Thanks,' she said.

'Thank you,' he replied.

She smiled. 'No. For coming round so quickly, without asking questions or reminding me it was the middle of the night.'

'I was flattered that you thought of ringing me first, before anyone else,' he said.

Debs felt her colour rise. 'I just thought I could trust you,' she said. 'And that you'd know what to do.'

'You can, Debs,' he said, his face turning serious again. 'Though I'm not sure I can promise I'll always know what to do so easily.'

And then he was gone. Debs watched him walk over to his car, then disappear inside. Only when his van turned the corner and his engine was no longer within hearing distance did she close the door.

Isobel arrived around tea-time the same day to pick Abbie up. As a thank-you gift she presented Debs with an exquisite ivory silk shawl.

'But you're paying me for looking after Abbie!' Debs protested. 'There's no need to buy me presents, too!'

'You deserve it,' Isobel said, 'for not

saying I told you so, when I explained what happened in Madrid. You were suspicious of Robby from the start. You could have rubbed my nose in it, but you haven't.

Debs wandered over to the window and held the shawl up to the light in order to appreciate it better. It was far too elegant to wear to any of the places she ever went. From her position, she could see Jim at Isobel's front door, busy changing the lock. He'd been at the house a good hour now and when he'd finished he'd promised to pop over to say hello. Already she was getting butterflies at the prospect. She turned her attention back to Isobel's words.

'We all make mistakes with men,' she said, instantly banishing the thought that has she herself might be on the verge of committing one with Jim.

Isobel sighed. 'But I seem to have a rare talent for it,' she said. 'It what comes of having been in love with the Romantic poets since the age of sixteen. Who can ever shape up by comparison?'

'Well, you don't seem as devastated

about breaking up with Robby as I'd imagined,' Debs said.

'Put it down to experience,' Isobel replied. 'It was never a long-term thing, Rob and me. It was fun, that's all. Until it stopped being fun, that is.'

★　★　★

' 'Fun, till it stopped being fun,' was what she said,' Debs repeated to Jim later, as they sat drinking tea in her kitchen for the second time in twenty-four hours.

'Well, he won't be able to get back in now, if he tries to again tonight,' Jim said. 'What d'you suppose it was he was after? Just chancing his arm, d'you think seeing if Isobel had got any more valuables stashed away? Or was it something specific he was looking for?'

'What sort of something?'

Jim shrugged. 'No idea,' he said. 'But if he was mixed up in drugs . . . '

He trailed off, and turned his attention to the toasted sandwich Debs had just made him. She pondered Jim's words. An image of the guy who'd been looking for

Robby suddenly popped into her head and she was struck with the same unease she'd felt when he'd tapped her on the shoulder yesterday. She gave an involuntary shiver.

'You all right?' Jim asked her.

She nodded. 'Lack of sleep, that's all.'

'Tell me about it,' he laughed 'Brilliant toastie, by the way.'

Sleep came easily to Debs that night. She was looking forward to tomorrow, and seeing Chelsea again. And, of course, she'd see Jim, too, at Ed's this time. Ed was one of her clients, a nice old gent. How different it would be from last week. After their initial surprise at bumping into each other for the second time, and her long-winded explanation about what she was doing at Ed's house, they'd gone about their work ignoring each other but for the odd smile or nod of acknowledgement. Earlier, sitting at her kitchen table, Jim had asked her if she'd like to go out to for a meal on Saturday evening.

At first she'd hesitated. She hadn't seen Chelsea for a week. They had a lot of catching up to do. But then she checked herself. This week away from her daughter had ended up being a good thing in the end. She'd got some practice in at being herself, and not just Chelsea's mum, which is how she'd seen herself for so long now.

She'd have the best part of the weekend and all next week to catch up with her. Besides, what was the betting that as soon as Chelsea crossed the threshold she'd be on the phone to her friends, arranging how soon she could meet up with them to tell them all about her adventures in Switzerland.

'I'd love to come,' she'd said finally. And it was impossible not to notice how pleased Jim looked, and to be pleased herself, that her saying yes was so important to him.

The shrill ringing of the telephone woke her abruptly. A quick glance at her bedside clock revealed it to be two in the morning. Who on earth could be ringing her at this hour? she wondered, staggering out of bed and grabbing her dressing gown before groping her way to the landing and downstairs to the hall.

'Mum? Is that you?'

Chelsea's voice was no more than a whisper.

'Chelsea? What on earth's the matter? Is everything all right?'

'It will be once I'm back home.' There was a tremor in her voice that threatened to overwhelm her.

Debs could feel herself getting angry already. Tony was at the bottom of this, she was certain.

'I didn't want to phone before because I knew it would only upset you and then it would have upset me even more,' she went on. 'But I'm so angry after what Molly told me tonight when I put her to bed that I've not been able to sleep.' There was a beat, before she added, 'Did I wake you, by the way?'

'It doesn't matter, love. Just tell me what's been going on.'

As Chelsea's tale unfolded, Debs found herself growing more and more furious with Tony and his new wife and more and more sorry for Chelsea. That she should find out, from a four-year-old child, that the only reason she'd been invited on

116

holiday was because the latest in a long line of au pairs had had a strop and walked out on the family was monstrous!

'So that's what I've been. A surrogate au pair. I've hardly seen the side of a mountain or the outside of this chalet for the entire week,' Chelsea finished by saying.

'Oh, Chelsea. I'm so sorry.' Debs could fine no more words to say.

'It's not your fault, Mum. And I feel better now for getting it off my chest. And I'll be home tomorrow, too!'

It was as if their roles had suddenly become reversed, Debs thought, with Chelsea delivering upbeat little sound bites down the line in a bid to cheer her up.

'Listen,' Chelsea said, 'I think there's someone coming. I'd better go. This must be costing them a fortune.'

'Good,' Debs croaked, realising that this was the one and only time she'd ever expressed her real feelings for Tony in front of their daughter. Well, from now on, the gloves were off and if he ever rang up again with any more great ideas he knew exactly where he could shove them.

'I'll see you tomorrow, then,' Chelsea said. 'Love you.'

Debs stood staring at the receiver for some moments before she replaced it. Her fury had driven all ideas of sleep away. A cup of tea. That's what she needed. She shivered and drew her dressing gown around her tightly. Where was that draught coming from? It was almost as if there was a window open somewhere downstairs, or a door maybe. But that was ridiculous. She'd locked up earlier tonight, just like she did every night.

She caught the smell of tobacco mixed with something sweeter and spun round to find its source, her skin prickling with an anticipation that was quickly turning into fear. A figure, short, stocky, dressed in black from head to foot, rushed towards her. Instinctively, she raised her arms to ward off the crunching blow that, with a sickening certainty, she knew was coming her way any second now. As she sank to her knees, ears ringing and pain scything through her back and shoulders, she caught a glimpse of something pink and fluffy.

* * *

Ed was anxious. He'd been up and down at the window every two minutes for nearly an hour now. Where was Debs? She was never late. Half past nine, every Friday. You could set your clock by her.

It crossed his mind that he might somehow have upset her the last time she was here. He'd meant no offence by his remark that she was a fine-looking woman and that he was certain Jim, the handyman, thought so, too. A few years ago, any woman would have been flattered to hear herself called attractive. But times had changed and so had women from what he read in the papers and saw on TV and maybe he should have known better. He was an old fool, that was the top and bottom of it, meddling in other folk's business.

The knock at the back door raised his hopes and he scuttled off to answer it. But it was only Jim, come to fix the

119

guttering as he'd promised.

'You were expecting me, weren't you, Ed?' Jim hovered at the door, looking anxious. 'Only you look disappointed.'

'No. Come in. Come in. Do.'

'What's up? Anything I can help you with?'

He cast about for a space on the kitchen table where Ed's breakfast things still lay, before setting down his toolbox.

'It's Debs,' Ed said. 'She should have been here an hour ago, but there's no sign of her and she's not rung to let me know what's wrong.'

Jim furrowed his brow.

'She's never late and the one time she was ill she rang to explain why she wouldn't be in a good hour before she was even expected.' Ed was becoming more agitated with every word. 'I'm worried something might have happened to her. An accident, or something. I've got her address, Jim. I wonder . . . '

But Jim was already halfway out the door.

★   ★   ★

Debs was cold. She seemed to have lost her duvet but, when she reached out to locate it, her fingers made contact with a rough, hard surface instead of the warm, feathery softness she'd expected. In her confusion, she panicked and struggled to get up, but even the smallest movement sent a tidal wave of excruciating pain flooding through her body. It was a blessed relief to stop floundering and simply surrender herself to it, mind and body, until it washed her way to unconsciousness. She was OK lying here. She'd get her duvet later. Right now everything was all just too much trouble.

* * *

The police officer was being very patient with her.

'If it's too much for you, Mrs Randall, I can always come back later. You've had a nasty blow on the head and perhaps your memory's playing tricks on you.'

Debs sighed and closed her eyes. He was very sweet, this policeman, but he looked about Chelsea's age and, just like a teenager, he thought he knew better than she did about what had happened to her last night.

True, she didn't remember enough to given an accurate description of the thug who'd done this, and she'd had no idea, until they told her, how long she'd lain there on the landing, until Jim, at poor Ed's behest, had discovered her drifting in and out of consciousness. But she did remember that Abbie's teddy had been involved somewhere in among all this.

'It was the thing I saw when I went down,' she said again, feeling quite agitated now.

She wished Jim were with her. He'd believe her, she was sure, and he'd give this young whippersnapper a lesson in respecting his elders, too, into the bargain. But Jim was at her house, putting it to rights, or so he'd told her, when she'd eventually been allowed to see him. Hopping mad he'd been, when he'd seen the state of her bruises and her arm in a sling. It was no use telling him that it looked worse than it felt, thanks to the painkillers.

'You make sure you get whoever did

this,' he'd said to the police officer, hardly able to contain his fury.

'We'll certainly do our best, sir,' the police officer had replied. And Jim had given him a look that could only be interpreted as meaning that if they didn't then they'd have him to answer to.

A pretty, young nurse popped her head round the door of the side room where Debs had been allocated a bed.

'Still giving you the third degree, is he?' she said, holding her head coquettishly to one side — for the policeman's benefit, obviously, Debs thought.

The PC kept his eyes firmly on his note-pad, but the blush creeping up his cheeks wasn't lost on Debs.

'Only you've got two visitors and they won't take no for an answer,' she went on.

And then the room was filled with the biggest bouquet of flowers that Debs had ever seen and here was Isobel, peering from behind it, her face all concern. And bringing up the rear was Chelsea. Chelsea! She was back today and here was she in a hospital bed instead of being at home to greet her. She struggled to sit up, and then fell back on to her pillow with a wince of pain.

'No, don't try to move,' Chelsea cried, rushing over to her bedside and practically sending the poor PC flying.

Debs' fragile state curtailed Chelsea's ability to hug her somewhat. But she quickly found her mother's hand and it was obvious to Debs and everyone else present that she had no intention of letting go unless the two of them were prised apart.

'When did you get back to England and how are you?' Debs asked.

Between them, in a tumble of words, Isobel and Chelsea explained that Jim had been at the house, making good the lock her intruder had forced, when Chelsea — dropped off at the door by her dad, who'd immediately sped away — had arrived. Once she'd heard the story, she'd run straight round to Isobel's to ask her to take her to the hospital. Debs wanted to ask about Switzerland, and to find out more about what had happened there. But that was private, between the two of them, and it would have to wait till they were alone.

'Have you found out who did this yet?' Chelsea said, acknowledging the policeman at last.

Nervously, he explained that they were only now for the first time going over the events. Debs was beginning to feel sorry for the poor boy, swamped by so much oestrogen in one small room.

'I was just describing my attacker,' Debs said. 'Stocky, wearing black from head to foot. Couldn't see his face. He was carrying Abbie's pink teddy. I'd brought it from Isobel's house for Abbie to play with, only I was told she was scared of it, so I hid it so she wouldn't find it, just like I said, officer. Only you seem to think that this bump on the head has sent me gaga.'

The PC shifted in his seat, uncomfortably. Chelsea and Isobel changed amused glances, which only made Debs dig her heels in further.

'He had it in his hand and then he dropped it when he came at me,' she insisted.

'So he broke in just to steal Abbie's

teddy?' Chelsea said. 'Weird!'

'Oh. My. God.' Isobel had gone white.

All three locked at her in expectation.

'I should have guessed,' she said. 'You told me you found it in the spare room when I was certain I'd hidden it right at the bottom of the toy box.'

Debs and Isobel locked eyes.

'Robby,' they both said in unison.

★   ★   ★

Debs was back home, still creaky and still bruised, but triumphant after her story of the teddy had finally been accepted. It had played on her mind, Isobel told the PC back at the hospital, right from the moment Debs told her where she'd found it, just as she'd been about to leave for Madrid, because she knew for certain that she hadn't put it there.

And if she hadn't put it there, then someone else must have. And that someone else had to be Robby. She didn't know why he'd put it there. But put it there he had, and when he'd come to retrieve it he'd been unable to find it again. Which was why he'd come out of Isobel's empty-handed in the middle of the night, Debs had added. Extremely lucidly, she thought, for one who only five minutes previously had been considered by all as mad as a hatter.

'So, this — Robby,' the PC said. 'Do you think he did this to you?'

Oh, no, it wasn't Robby. Too short, too stocky for Robby.

⋆ ⋆ ⋆

'Now, are you sure you don't mind me going out with Jim tonight?'

'Mum, I've got four of my mates coming round,' Chelsea protested. 'You absolutely must go out. I've got so much to tell them and I don't want you here stealing the limelight.'

Debs laughed. Chelsea's ghastly trip to Switzerland was a thing of the past. She doubted it would even raise a mention tonight. Everything paled into insignificance next to what had been happening in this very street over the last seven days.

'How do I look?' she asked Chelsea,

throwing her new shawl round her shoulder.

'Like a battered wife. Though not as bad as Robby, poor thing.'

Pictures of Robby had appeared on the front page of the local newspaper. He'd been given a much worse battering than Debs for upsetting the drug dealer for whom he'd been forced to hold a gun as a way of repaying his debts, then later been unable to locate it, according to the press.

'Don't be giving him your sympathy,' Debs said. 'If he'd have knocked on my door and asked for the teddy I'd have given it to him. Instead he had to get some other lowlife to come round and beat me up for it.'

'Suppose you're right.'

'I know I am.'

'So, where is it to be tonight? Posh restaurant?'

Debs could see Jim's van turning the corner. Not a posh restaurant, no. Not with her face looking like a piece of Stilton from the cheeseboard. Jim was cooking for her tonight. He wanted to pamper her, he'd said. If she was agreeable.

She was definitely agreeable to a bit of pampering, she said. And she loved home cooking, too. There was always the small problem of the washing-up afterwards, of course. But tonight she had the feeling that the washing-up was going to have to wait. Quite a long time.

Murder at St Martin's

1

'No, I'm sorry, Alasdair. I really can't tell you *where* he is.'

When Lynda Drew recognised the quavering, almost ecclesiastical tones of Alasdair Craig, the Deputy Headmaster — The Crag, as he was know to the boys and, behind his back, to many of the staff, too — she rather wished she'd followed her instincts and let the phone ring.

'Well, perhaps *you* can help,' Alasdair said, 'It's about the flowers for this afternoon's portrait unveiling ceremony.'

Lynda fixed her eyes on her tired reflection in the mirror, just above the telephone table. One of these days, she swore, she'd take it down and replace it with a framed picture.

Maybe she should have asked Saskia Kennedy to knock one off for her in her free time, when she wasn't so busy getting Mason to sit for her. A nice little seascape, maybe. Or a big bowl of fruit.

Anyway, too late now, thank God. After today, she'd be out of their lives for ever.

It was a tradition here at St Martin's for every Principal to have his portrait painted before he retired. Mason had come up with the idea of commissioning his portrait to coincide with the school centenary celebrations. That way there would be double the press coverage.

A stroke of genius, Lynda had to admit, until she'd seen the portrait, which, to her mind at least, was hardly flattering. That was Mason for you, though. Didn't matter if he looked like the back end of a bus. To have one's portrait painted conferred status. And he was all for that.

Besides, it was different for men. Nobody cared about a man's lines and wrinkles. Not if you were headmaster of such a prestigious boys' school as St Martin's, single-handedly responsible for turning round its fortunes, so that these days there was a waiting list parents would trample over each other to get on to.

Alasdair was still wittering on. He enjoyed nothing better than to complain how hard done by he was.

'It's too bad of him to go AWOL at a time like this,' he said. 'There's so much to be done and I'm at a complete loss about where to start.'

That was unsurprising. Alasdair had been left out of the loop on this one. She, on the other hand, could quote the order of this afternoon's events verbatim. She'd overheard Mason going over the details with the Bursar on the phone enough times recently.

Easel to be set up previous night and portrait installed and covered ready for the unveiling at fifteen hundred hours the following day. Flowers to be arranged during the morning. Tea to be ready for serving at sixteen hundred hours on the lawn, weather permitting. If not, in the Masters' Dining Room. Mini quiches, sandwiches, scones and fancies. And a big cake for the centenary celebration, of course. Mustn't forget that. Candles, icing, the works. Happy 200th, St Martin's. And, for God's sake, apostrophe or The Crag will never the let me forget it.

If public events brought out the worst in Alasdair, Mason thrived on them. This afternoon would be all about him — which was exactly as he liked it. Though she hadn't seen anything written down, she could just imagine what his speech would be like.

It would be the usual mix of wisdom and self-deprecating wit that always succeeded in winning over his audience. He would insist that the portrait was simply too flattering. And, no doubt, he'd wax eloquent about the skill of Saskia ruddy Kennedy, the artist who'd painted it — vastly over-rated in Lynda's opinion. She'd be there, of course, looking gorgeous as usual.

'You would tell me if you were fielding Mason's calls, wouldn't you?'

'Honestly, Alasdair. If I knew where he was, I'd tell you!'

The man was insufferable. For someone so secretive about his own private life, he was remarkably nosey about other people's. Perhaps she ought to ask him if Yvonne was still managing to stay sober after that incident at last year's staff Christmas party, and see how *he* liked it!

'Look, Alasdair. Just sign for the flowers. Then turn up in the hall this afternoon at three. That's really all you need to do.' she said. 'Now, if you'll excuse me, I need to start thinking about getting ready myself.'

Maybe ten, well, fifteen years ago, she'd have made a pretty picture, she thought as she caught another glimpse of herself in the mirror. But not now. Without putting too fine a point on it, she was past her sell-by date. If she was going to look anything like human by three o'clock, she was going to have to work on her face without delay.

★   ★   ★

Luke Drew woke that morning with a banging head and — not unusually — Saskia's name running through it. In the other bed, snoring lightly, jaw on chest, Oscar, his roommate, lay on his back, beefy arms flung out, sleeping the sleep of the mentally unencumbered.

Life was simple for the Oscars of this world, Luke thought, as he pulled his duvet over his head. Sleep, food, rugger in winter, cricket in summer and a bit of

137

prep tagged on at the end of the day, but never enough to tax the brain. If only it were that simple.

He longed for his own room. Communal living had never been his thing. Couldn't stand other people's mess for one thing or being interrupted when he was in the middle of a good book.

Worse was the pretence. Making out you fancied one of those giggly Year Elevens from St Faith's down in the town, with their pelmet skirts and too much eye make-up, and having to listen to all the smutty talk about them.

Was it any wonder that he kept a distance whenever the conversation turned to Saskia? Just the thought of them talking about her like she was one more piece of meat made his blood boil. He had to keep his distance or they'd soon know how he felt about her. Boys hunted in packs. If he came to her defence just once they'd sniff him out straight off and then he'd never hear the end of it. The one spark on the horizon was that next year he'd be in the Upper Sixth and entitled to a room of his own.

'If you want privacy, then you can always haul your stuff over to the cottage and take up residence with your aged parents,' his mother had said, last time he'd complained about the archaic boarding rules at St Martin's.

Mothers! Honestly, they just didn't get it. Bad enough being the Headmaster's son. God only knows how they'd treat him if he started claiming privileges and rubbing everyone's noses in the fact that any time he liked he could walk out of here, through the quad, and be home in two minutes. No, he'd have to put up with it till next year when he'd legitimately be entitled to a room of his own. He couldn't wait.

He could murder a glass of water. And somewhere in his drawer, he knew there were painkillers. Maybe he should get up and sort himself out before this headache got any worse. Double Chemistry first two with Brock meant there was no chance he'd be able to get away with keeping his head down at the back of the class.

His thoughts returned to the previous night. What if that policewoman changed her mind and investigated a bit more closely? It'd be all over for him, his dad being who he was.

Caught — not only with fake ID for which he'd had to fork out fifteen quid. But drinking in a pub, too. He'd broken school rules — *only Upper Sixth formers eighteen years of age to be allowed in public houses and only if accompanied by a master* — and the law of the land as well. And on top of the threat of his father's wrath hanging over his head, after today, he would probably never see Saskia again. He didn't know which part of his life he hated most.

★ ★ ★

'Posh kids. They're a mystery to me.' WPC Tracy Coppard inched her tray along, trying to decide between a cottage cheese salad and an all-day breakfast. It was a no-brainer, if truth were told.

'Those boys from St Martin's up to their high jinks again?' Her friend, WPC Sharon Smith, looked to be going for the salad, but snatched back her hand at the last second. 'Good girl,' Tracey thought. 'That's clinched it, then.'

'We can always start the diet tomorrow.' Sharon flashed her a cheeky grimace.

'You've twisted my arm.'

'So, you were telling me a story.'

The two colleagues eventually found a table that wasn't full of other people's leavings and sat down at it. They had half an hour before they were back on duty. Hardly any time at all to draw breath, actually. But it was no use complaining. Criminals didn't keep office hours.

'Yeah, last night. I was puppy-walking Gary, that rookie PC.'

'Gary, eh?' Sharon speared a chip and posted it into her large mouth. 'Don't know about you, but I certainly would!'

Honestly, Sharon could be very coarse at times. Not to mention desperate. That Gary was a babe-in-arms. You only had to look at him to see the type of girl he went for. Sharon had no chance. Probably wouldn't stop her trying. Never usually did.

'Do you want to hear what happened or not?'

'All right. Keep your hair on.'

Now that she had Sharon's undivided attention, Tracy continued her story.

'I took him round the town. Pointed out the landmarks, the short cuts, the places never to go unless you had back-up.'

It didn't take long — Lumbermouth-on-Sea was hardly the Bronx. There were the usual suspects, of course — most of whom lived on the Lighthouse Estate, a place Tracy was all too familiar with, unfortunately. And in summer, there were always a few incidents down on the beach. But nothing major had ever occurred on Tracy's beat and probably never would, if statistics were anything to go by.

'Anyway. We were walking along the top road with the sea below us, heading back to the station, when Gary spots this lad stumbling along the beach.'

'Sharp eyes,' Sharon interrupted. Was she already making an inventory of his plus points? Tracy wondered. She'd be giving him a hearing test next. Asking him to open his mouth so she could check his teeth.

'It was getting dark quite quickly, even while we stood there watching him. Gary was for running down the steps right away and finding out what was going on with the lad. Kid was all over the place and, fair enough, he might have been injured in some way.'

She'd had to lay a hand on Gary's arm to restrain him, actually. Straining at the leash, he was. That was the trouble with men. If you could call Gary a man. It was a moot point. They always wanted to get stuck in, that was their trouble. There was a lot to be said for just watching and waiting.

'Seemed to be having a conversation with someone, which started to get me a bit worried. If he was having paranoid delusions then he'd better be having them under the trained eye of a psychiatric doctor, was what I thought.'

Sharon agreed.

'Anyway, it was when he fell over we both decided that enough was enough. What with the tide coming in.'

'So what did you find?'

'Posh boy. Drunk on two pints. Or so

143

he said. He was probably telling the truth.'

'Lightweight,' Sharon said, with a chuckle. 'I'm guessing he was a Martini and not a St Bede's kid? Most of the Year Elevens at St Bede's can even drink *me* under the table.'

'I would think so. I probably should have asked. But, I dunno. Something held me back. I felt sorry for him, I think.'

Sharon looked puzzled. 'Not like you, Trace. We've all heard your views on public schools.'

'I know. I must be going soft in my old age,' she said. 'Must be partly to do with how terrified he looked when he saw me and Gary. I'm used to evils and back-chat from kids his age whenever you pull them up on something. But this kid was different. Proper manners, you know. It would have been too easy to make an example of him.'

'Very philosophical,' Sharon said. 'On his own, did you say?'

Tracy nodded. 'Out solo for the evening like little Billy No-Mates. No alcohol on his person, so all I can guess is that either he started drinking before he came out or someone had been serving him illegally.'

'That's not possible, is it?'

'False ID. All the kids are on to it. There's only so much investigating a landlord's prepared to do when he's busy.'

And only so much investigating Lumbermouth-on-Sea Constabulary was prepared to do, too. What was one mildly intoxicated teenager compared to several off their heads, involved in a brawl up on the Lighthouse Estate?

If it hadn't been for that call coming through, she'd have insisted on escorting the boy all the way back to St Martin's and delivering him into the hands of the Headmaster. As it was, she contented herself with giving him a telling off.

'Kid got lucky,' Sharon said. 'How did you leave it?'

'Just told him to keep his nose clean. I won't be reporting you this time, I said, but if I catch you in this state again, rest assured, you'll be in trouble and not just with your headmaster.'

'I expect that's the end of that then,' Sharon said.

'I wouldn't be surprised,' Tracy agreed.

She hated to say it, but the boy was from a good home and in possession of a good education. The chances of him falling foul of the law compared with most of her usual clientele from the estate were microscopic. It wasn't *her* idea of a just society, but then she didn't make the rules.

'Come on, Shazz,' she said, scraping back her chair. 'Back to the beat, babes.'

* * *

Luke got out of bed, pulled on his clothes and let himself out as quietly as possible so as not to disturb the sleeping Oscar. A brisk walk would clear his head. That's what his dad always said after he'd been at the school claret. Although lately, of course, so Mum said, he'd swapped walking for jogging.

'Ridiculous for a man of his age,' she'd grumbled at him.

Sometimes Mum forgot she was talking to her son. He suspected it was because she was short of female friends here at the school. There was Matron, of course, and the Bursar and The Crag's wife. 'That lush', as Mum called her.

But she didn't seem to be inclined to mix with any of them. Maybe she felt the same as he did — that people were suspicious of you just because of your status so the best way of dealing with that was to keep your distance.

Dad, on the contrary, took chumminess to an art form. Everyone, from the lowliest dinner lady to visiting government ministers, seemed to fall under his spell. Luke had spent a long time wondering just how he managed to pull it off. But all he'd come up with so far was this. Either you were born that way or you weren't and if you weren't then, try as you might, you'd always feel awkward around other people.

The first time he'd met Saskia, he'd felt awkward; sitting round the dining table — it was a Saturday evening and he'd been 'let out' for the weekend. She was so exquisitely beautiful, for one thing. Like a doll. Small, perfectly proportioned with an urchin haircut that should have made her look butch, but, in fact, made her look feminine.

But his awkwardness hadn't lasted long. The way she'd included him in the conversation — asking his opinion, laughing at his feeble attempt at a joke, complimenting him when his father let slip he was applying to Oxford next year — all of these things had given him confidence. And for the first time in his life, he felt like an adult. A real man. Falling in love with a beautiful woman.

Crazy, but it was as if just thinking about Saskia had carried him in the direction of the small cottage on the cliff that overlooked the sea, in which she'd taken up residence for the summer term — the amount of time she'd been allocated to paint Dad's portrait.

This afternoon — in less than eight hours, in fact — his father's portrait would finally be unveiled. Later it would join those of all the other past Heads of St Martin's. After today there would be no need for Saskia to remain in Lumbermouth. She'd be off. Back to London. And all he'd have of her were those photos on his camera, sneakily snapped when she'd been unaware of his presence.

Someone was coming out of the cottage. Two people. Saskia, pulling her dressing gown tightly around her tiny frame to ward off the early morning chill. Leaning towards a taller, male figure, putting her arms around his neck and pulling his face to hers.

The sight sent him reeling like a blow to the stomach. He felt the bile rise in his throat and beads of perspiration spring from his brow, and had to steady himself against the tree trunk he'd been hiding behind. His father. Kissing Saskia. And in that ridiculous tracksuit.

He couldn't stay and witness another second of this revolting display. Turning on his heel, he dipped out of sight and ran as fast as he could back to school.

* * *

It was three-twenty as Alasdair Craig nervously made his way to the podium. Row upon row of boys in the neat maroon uniform of St Martin's, who'd been growing ever more restless during the half hour they'd been sitting down, went silent.

Alasdair had been fielding enquiries as to Mason's whereabouts since noon, simply recounting the information Lynda — somewhat reluctantly, he thought — had given him. Namely that Mason had risen early and gone for a run, without taking his mobile.

Since then he'd been clutching at increasingly feeble straws. Today was Mason's Big Day — it was *his* portrait that was about to be unveiled, after all. Surely he ought to be here to unveil it?

He'd even suggested ringing the local hospital. Or sending out a search party to look for him. Maybe Mason had fallen somewhere and now lay injured, unable to move. Well, yes, they definitely ought to do the former, the Chair of Governors agreed, his beady eye on the hall clock. But everyone was here. The cake was ready. The local MP had booked today months ago and would be quite unable to return for at least another two months.

'I really think you ought to step in,

Deputy Head,' he'd insisted, as if he hadn't heard a word Alasdair had said. Clearly, there was no way out.

Once on stage, Alasdair raced through his preamble, apologising for the delay, which was unavoidable. But the show must go on, since many of the important guests had travelled far to attend. He made a sweeping gesture with his arm, taking in Saskia Kennedy, who looked as stunning as ever in one of those complicated outfits she always wore. She smiled at him graciously, which gave him the confidence to think he was doing the right thing.

'And so,' he concluded, fingers poised at the edge of the crimson cloth, 'it is my great pleasure to unveil this latest portrait which is soon to adorn the walls of the Master's dining room, Headmaster Mason Drew, the twentieth serving headmaster, on the founding date of our beloved school, St Martin's.'

It was a collision of events. An expectant hush descended as the piece of silk floated to the ground. The silence lingered, but thickened in texture as if the whole room held its breath then exhaled as one shocked body.

Alasdair Craig swung round at the unexpected sound. He couldn't believe what he was seeing. It was the Head's portrait all right, but it had been cruelly defaced, scored repeatedly with a sharp object so it was almost impossible to distinguish Mason's features.

And then the heavy oak doors of the hall swung open. As soon as he saw the policewoman and the plainclothes officer accompanying her, he was gripped by a grim sense of foreboding.

All eyes fixed themselves on the pair and you could have heard a pin drop and Alasdair ordered the masters to lead the boys out of the hall immediately. As they reluctantly filed out, heads craned, Alasdair hurried towards the uninvited guests. But it seemed they weren't remotely interested in him. They'd found the person they were looking for. Lynda.

And now they were leaning towards her. The female officer was speaking in a quiet, respectful voice. He watched the colour drain from Lynda's face and heard her pitiful wail rise up and fill the room.

'No! It can't be true!' She cried, before she staggered to the ground.

But Alasdair knew it was. Mason Drew was dead.

2

Earlier that morning, Luke had pulled his denim jacket around him for protection against the chill. He was starting to get hungry, but none of the cafés along the pier were open yet. Besides, he had no money. He'd come out on impulse, to clear his head, with the intention of being back ready for first period. But that was before he'd seen what he'd seen. No way was he going back now, whatever trouble he got into for it. If he had any money, he knew exactly what he'd do. Buy more booze.

Hair of the dog, his father called it. It might have gone some way to obliterating the memory of his father embracing Saskia at the door of her cottage, still in her dressing gown, as if . . . No, he had no intentions of even going there.

He chose the short cut to the beach down the dizzyingly steep steps, risking slipping on the wet stone but not really caring. Clumps of seaweed washed up by the waves floated like dead eels along the water's edge. Down here there wasn't a soul in sight, but, dotted on the horizon, cargo ships hovered beneath the sea mist, creeping him out just as they always did with their ghostly silhouettes.

Saskia, Saskia. How could she do that to him? And with his own father, too? The wind against his face was salty damp. When he put his hand up to dry his face, it mingled with his own salt tears.

★ ★ ★

Yvonne Craig had been lying when she told her husband how sorry she was not to be able to attend Drew's thing this afternoon. *Oh, do keep up, Alasdair*, she'd said, over the toast and marmalade, when he'd expressed a mix of surprise and irritation at her announcement.

That glimmer of relief in his eyes hadn't escaped her, either, no matter how well he'd imagined he'd disguised it. In the past, she'd made no effort to conceal her feelings about attending school events. They bored her silly. If she wasn't coming, then he'd be able to enjoy himself much more.

The real reason for her reluctance to attend the portrait unveiling wouldn't have even occurred to him. Alasdair was constitutionally unable to see further than the end of his nose and Mason was far too much of a gentleman to rub his nose in the fact that his wife was fast becoming a public embarrassment.

Since that little incident at the Christmas party, she couldn't bear to be in the same room as Mason and would have gone to any lengths to avoid him. Thank God for her imaginary friend.

Ann, remember? Oldest school chum? Recently widowed? Needs taking out of herself — new puppy — perfect solution. She'd arranged it months ago, before there was any mention of a portrait, let alone an unveiling.

It had helped tremendously that Alasdair's head had been so full of rubbish about flowers and signatures and portrait unveilings, not to mention conspiracy theories concerning Lynda Drew, whom he'd just now on the phone more or less accused of lying when she said she had no idea of Mason's whereabouts. And then, after slamming it back down, criticising the Bursar, whom he accused — this time to Yvonne herself — of trying to upstage him.

Just in case he hadn't fallen for it so easily, she'd prepared a stack of reasons as to why her little outing had to be today of all days. Inoculations. Vet. Certificate. The all-clear on Ann's shingles. But, in the end, thanks to Alasdair's paranoia, she hadn't needed to use any of them.

She'd spent the day driving, looking round the shops, sitting in cafés staring out of the window, and watching the hours tick away. When three o'clock came round, she pictured Mason strolling up to the podium, confidently delivering his speech, full of the well-received ad libs he'd doubtless have sweated blood over.

Then, once that was over, doing the rounds, shaking everyone's hand and sharing a joke with them; keeping an eye out for her, so he could do his best to avoid her, perhaps. Maybe he'd taken

Lynda to one side — had a quiet word, husband to wife. *For God's sake. Keep the sherry away from that woman. I don't want her throwing herself at me again like she did at the Christmas party.*

Just the memory of the incident brought her blood rushing to her cheeks. The shame of it! At the time, she'd been so confident she'd had Mason's attention. Convinced herself he'd been glancing her way at the top table. Why else had she made a beeline for him later? Drink, and the stupid tricks it played on her judgment, was why.

What was it they had chatted about? She'd spent hours searching her memory but was still stumped. Except that he'd laughed at her jokes, brought his head closer to listen to her, even touched her arm occasionally, all signs he found her fascinating company. Sober, she understood the truth behind those gestures. The touch on her arm was to steady her. His lips on her ear was his way of not drawing attention to the fact that he was telling her he thought she'd had enough and it might be better if she rejoined Alasdair quietly before

158

she drew any more attention from the other guests.

It was dark now and the celebrations would have been over long ago. As she drove up the long, winding drive to the school, Yvonne quenched all thoughts of Mason. It was time to turn her thoughts to puppies — made-up ones.

★   ★   ★

Alasdair Craig sat at his desk in his study, staring out of the window on to the empty playing field. He should probably go home. Yvonne would be back soon from whichever old girlfriend she was visiting this week and would be surprised not to find him there.

She'd be bound to ring him to find out what was going on and then he'd have to tell her everything. Or everything he knew, at least, which wasn't very much at all. Mason had been shot. Somewhere in the middle of the golf course. Dressed for a run. And then the portrait — so terribly defaced. It was inconceivable, all of it. Like something from a movie.

She really ought to find out from him, not from some random passing Master or boy. The shock might be more than she could cope with. She would be bound to come rushing straight over and he didn't think his own nerves were up to dealing with one of Yvonne's theatrical turns on top of everything else that had happened. Far better to get over there and prepare for her arrival. Plump the cushions up a bit, pour her a drink.

But still he sat there, staring out of the window. If he needed an excuse not to go home tonight, then at least he had a good one. Sooner or later he could expect a visit from the police — that somewhat pneumatic WPC and the feral-looking Detective Inspector. *We'll want another word with you later, Sir,* he'd said. *So if you can make yourself accessible . . .*

They were obviously still far too busy with Lynda, who was no doubt deeply distressed by events and couldn't be left alone. He hoped someone had had the good sense to pop over to Luke's House and fetch him. At a time like this, mother and son needed each other.

Should *he* have been the one to do that? Alasdair searched his conscience. No, far better to leave it to his housemaster. How he hated all this. Unlike Mason, he hadn't come into teaching to be an administrator.

He gave a heartfelt sigh. This was the real reason for him remaining here, at his desk, if only he'd admit it. Once home, he knew exactly what to expect. Yvonne's shock at Mason's death and the disfigurement of his portrait, not to mention her sympathy for his family, would quickly fizzle out.

Before he could say, *Do you really need a top-up just yet?* she'd be straight on to her hobby horse. *A chance for you to get the headship at last, Alasdair!* And he'd hear nothing else until he begged her to show a bit of respect and drop the subject.

Although he'd been half expecting it, the sharp rap at the door made him jump. The police, it had to be. Yvonne never knocked.

'Come,' he called out imperiously.

They were both here. DI Kevin Platt

and WPC Tracy Coppard. He prided himself on his memory for names. Alasdair waved at a couple of chairs and they both sat down.

'How is poor Lynda?' he asked.

'As you'd expect,' the WPC said. 'Cut up.'

Her eyes ranged round the room, took in the book-lined walls and dusty pot plants and returned to his face. Clearly, she was not impressed by evidence of so much scholarliness. Probably never read anything more challenging than a Dan Brown novel, Alasdair decided.

'Of course.' He nodded, steepling his hands. 'And Luke. How's he taking it?'

The two officers exchanged puzzled glances.

'Mason's son,' he explained. 'Surely his housemaster has given him permission to go home?'

'We know nothing about any son, Sir,' the Inspector said. 'Mrs Drew is with her doctor. I believe she's been sedated. As you can imagine, all she was concerned about was what had happened to her husband.'

'Maybe you could ring his — what is it? — housemaster — and find out what's happening with the boy,' the WPC said. 'Don't seem right, him not being home.'

It was clear to Alasdair what this woman thought about public schools. They were elitist institutes, churning out the next members of the Establishment. If her vocabulary stretched to words longer than two syllables — *cut up*, indeed. More likely she preferred to think of them as schools full of posh twits.

'We don't lock boys up against their will these days, Officer,' Alasdair said, already reaching for the telephone.

The WPC arched her eyebrows slightly, as if she didn't really believe him, while the Inspector tapped his foot and waited for Alasdair to get through. The conversation with Luke's housemaster, Mr Digby-Jones, was brief yet baffling.

Wasn't Luke with his mother? a startled Digby-Jones asked. No, otherwise he wouldn't be ringing, replied Alasdair tartly. No, no, of course not, a chastened Digby-Jones replied. Though, now he came to think of it, he had no memory of seeing Luke in the hall at any time this afternoon. Was Mr Digby-Jones saying that Luke had missed the ceremony completely? demanded Alasdair.

The inscrutable expressions on the faces of the two police officers convinced Alasdair they'd already judged him and found him wanting. In response, he injected more vigour into his tone.

Could Mr Digby-Jones please take it upon himself to have a thorough look for the boy and get back to him as soon as possible, he demanded, before he put the phone down. There, let that show 'em who was in charge!

'I do hope you haven't formed the impression that the school is lax when it comes to keeping tabs on the where-abouts of our students,' he said. 'Only, as you can imagine, today has not been a typical day.'

'Not at all,' the Inspector said. 'As you said, you don't lock them up against their will these days.'

Alasdair couldn't be sure, but he thought he detected a snigger coming from the WPC. The phone burst into life again. Probably Digby-Jones getting back to him.

'Alasdair, I'm coming over. Stay where you are.' It was Yvonne.

* * *

Tracy Coppard would much rather have been out on that field with her friend, Sharon, and the other officers, combing the area where Mason Drew's body had been found. But as soon as she got the call from Mrs Drew's GP, she had to return to the Principal's house, where, as appointed family liaison officer, she would be expected to remain with Mrs Drew until her sister arrived from Surrey.

They'd get nothing from Mr Chips here. And now his hysterical wife had turned up, flapping her hands and shrieking like a banshee. She'd finally calmed down a bit and was sitting at her husband's side in a chair Platt had dragged over from the corner for her.

Let me get you a chair, Mrs Craig, he'd said, baring his teeth in a grotesque parody of a smile. She'd fluttered her eyelashes at him, loving the attention. Tracy knew the type. Fifteen years ago, when she'd been in her prime, someone had slapped a preservation order on her and she hadn't changed a thing about her appearance since. Nor her opinions, neither, probably.

Tracy couldn't understand what had got into the DI. Anybody could have murdered Mason Drew, including the two people sitting in this room with them. He should have had his scowl on. Not been playing out a scene from *Upstairs Downstairs* with the lady of the manor. Now he was asking if he could get her a glass of water!

'Maybe something a little stronger.' Mrs Craig eyed a glass-fronted cabinet on the adjacent wall. 'Just for the shock.'

Mr Chips was clearly none too happy with this particular request. He'd acted like the big I Am before, but as soon as his missus had flung open the door and made her entrance it was as if he'd started to shrink in his seat. Did his wife always have that effect on him? Tracy wondered.

She'd actually started to feel sorry for him. In a flash, she was on her feet, pouring out water from the crystal jug into a matching glass and thrusting it under Mrs Craig's nose.

DI Platt tugged at the tie round his neck, a gesture Tracy was familiar with. It meant it was time to talk business.

'Mr Craig,' he began. 'You may have heard the rumours about the manner in which Mr drew met his death.'

Alasdair Craig nodded miserably. 'He was shot, I believe.'

'With a rifle.'

Mrs Craig stifled a sob. *Oh, do shut up and drink your water*, Tracy longed to say.

'Really? I'd imagined a handgun. I don't know why. Too many TV cop shows, I expect.'

'I expect so,' the DI agreed. A pregnant pause followed. Then Platt dropped his bombshell. 'I believe St Martin's houses a small arsenal on its premises. Am I right, Mr Craig?'

Tracy thought Chips' eyes would pop right out of his head.

'You can't be serious!' Mrs Craig spoke for him. 'Surely you're not suggesting that one of our boys did this?'

'It's an absurd accusation.' Chips had found his voice at last. 'None of the boys have access to the guns. And it's hardly an arsenal, Inspector. More a cupboard.'

'You say potato . . . ' Tracy mused. If there was somewhere that offered storage space for a pile of rifles, what did it matter what it was called?

'So who does have access to it?'

There was a big bunch of keys on the desk. 'Anyone, if he left them lying around like that,' she thought. 'Cleaners, tea ladies, the caretaker, naughty boys here for a whacking . . . '

'I do, as Deputy Head, of course. Then there's the Bursar.'

'And don't forget the housemasters,' his wife reminded him.

'How many would that be?'

'Four.'

The list went on and on!

'And, of course, Mason. He has — had the key.'

'I'd like to see this . . . cupboard, Mr

Craig. Would you mind accompanying the WPC and myself?'

'Of course not.' He reached for the keys, then turned to his wife. 'Yvonne. Would you mind going back to the house while I deal with this?'

'Are you serious? You want me to go out there, in the dark, on my own? When there's a gunman on the loose?'

'I hardly think . . . ' the DI began, but Yvonne Craig was having none of it.

'I'm coming with you!' She jumped up from her chair and grabbed her husband's arm.

They all trooped out of the room, and followed the deputy head up several flights of stairs and through a warren of corridors until finally they were at their destination, which to the uninitiated could easily have been mistaken for a stationery cupboard.

'The key, please, Mr Craig.' The DI held out his hand impatiently, whereupon the Deputy Head dropped the entire bunch into it.

'I'm really not sure which is which,' he said apologetically. 'You see, I never have cause to come up here. Perhaps I should have explained downstairs that, actually, no one does. The boys used to shoot — or some of them did — back in the days before Mason arrived as Principal.'

'The bad old days, eh?' his wife trilled.

The deputy head bristled.

'When was that?' the DI asked.

'Five years ago now. He put a stop to it. Saw it as sending out the wrong message to the parents. Made us look as though all we cared about were the sporting pursuits of the ruling class. The school had a great many problems before Mason Drew was appointed, Inspector.'

'Indeed. He was our saviour,' his wife put in. 'Put us right back on the academic map.'

Was there a note of sarcasm in her voice? Tracy wondered.

Alasdair Craig's phone started ringing.

'Digby-Jones,' he mouthed. 'I really need to take this.'

'Of course,' the Inspector said. 'Meanwhile, I'll keep on trying these keys.'

'Let me,' Tracy volunteered, stepping forward.

Tracy zipped through the bunch of keys in no time.

'Voila!' she said, when finally, and typically, the last one was found to work. The door sprang open.

She saw immediately that there was a space which should have contained a weapon.

The DI had seen it, too. 'I'm going to have to get Forensics over here right away,' he said.

For once, Mrs C was keeping quiet. Then Mr C, who'd taken himself a few yards off to take his call, reappeared. He looked dreadful, Tracy thought.

'It appears that Luke has been out of school all day,' he said, in a half-whisper.

Tracy caught the DI's eye. He raised one eyebrow enigmatically.

'I should go back to the house,' Tracy said at once. 'He may have heard the news and gone back there. Has he played truant before, this boy?' She asked.

Craig shook his head. The implications of Luke's disappearing act were beginning to dawn on everyone now.

'Take a stroll over there, Tracy,' the DI

said. 'No need to jump to conclusions just yet.'

★ ★ ★

'Ah! I was just about to call you. I have to leave now. Mrs Drew is asleep. I expect her to sleep through but if you have any concerns at all, please do ring me.'

The silver-haired GP handed Tracy his card, murmured his goodbyes and left, leaving Tracy alone to make her enquiries. Quickly, she checked every room but there was no sign of a teen boy anywhere.

What should she do now? Call it a day, or wait a little while. It was still only nine o'clock. Hardly curfew time. Yet, if he was responsible for his father's death, then he'd already had a head start on the police. He could be anywhere by now. Abroad, even.

Well, at least she could have a scout round the house to see if he'd taken his passport.

As she was crossing the hall to the study, the doorbell rang.

'Just a moment,' she called.

If this was Mrs Drew's sister coming from Surrey then she'd made good time.

It was a struggle to open the heavy oak door. But it wasn't Mrs Drew's sister. It was a boy. The same boy she'd had the run-in with last night, down on the beach.

'You!' she said. 'What are you doing here?'

He was obviously just as startled to see her as she was to see him.

'I'm Luke Drew,' he said. 'This is my house. But what are *you* doing here?'

3

Saskia Kennedy stood in the middle of her cluttered sitting room, deciding what to bin and what to put in storage till such time as she could have her work sent on. She'd done a lot of good sketches while she'd been here — besides *that* picture — and though she felt like setting fire to all of them right now, she didn't want to find herself regretting it a few months down the line when everything that had happened here at Lumbermouth was just a bad memory.

Take this one, for instance. She moved over to the window, all the better to study one particular group sketch. *Boys At Play*, she'd called it. One of a series, it was. There was definitely potential for a bigger work somewhere within these preliminary efforts.

A glimpse of blue serge on the cliff path distracted her from her purpose. Police, for sure. The place had been crawling

174

with them since yesterday afternoon.

As the police officer's footsteps approached, she dropped the sketch she'd been examining onto the nearest chair.

'Door's open,' she called out. She recognised the policewoman from yesterday. With that flame red hair and full figure she was definitely a pre-Raphaelite type. If only they'd met sooner. Saskia would have loved to paint her.

'Miss Kennedy? Tracy Coppard. I wonder if I could have a word.'

The officer walked cautiously over the threshold.

'Of course,' she said. 'Please. Just step over the artwork. This isn't a cottage, it's a Wendy house.'

'Looks like you're packing up,' the WPC replied.

'Detective material,' Saskia mused. 'Not.'

'What's to hang around for? My painting has been ruined. And I can hardly ask Mr Drew to sit for me again, can I?'

Immediately, her hand flew to her lips. 'Oh, dear. I'm rubbish at knowing what to say when disasters happen.'

'It's always awkward,' Tracy Coppard

said. 'And, actually, that's why I came over. To tell you you're free to go. You just need to leave your details in case we have to talk to you later.'

'Why would you need to do that?'

'Your portrait. Don't you want to find whoever it was that defaced it?'

'There are eight hundred boys in this school,' she said. 'Are you going to interview every single one of the little monsters?'

'We will if we need to,' Tracy said. 'Though it's hardly our priority at the moment.'

'Of course. Poor Mrs Drew. And Luke. How are they bearing up?'

'Mrs Drew's still sedated,' Tracy said. 'Luke doesn't seem to have caught up yet.'

'Shock,' Saskia said. 'It's a terrible thing to lose a parent when you're his age.'

'Sounds like you speak from personal experience, Miss Kennedy.'

'Please. Call me Saskia. And you're right. I lost my mother when I wasn't much older than Luke. And my father a couple of years ago.'

'I'm sorry.'

Saskia acknowledged Tracy's sympathy with a shrug. 'Look, I've got coffee. Why don't you stay and have a cup? If I can find a clean mug, that is. And you might have to move that if you want a seat,' she added, indicating the nearby chair with a glance.

The police officer picked up the sketch Saskia had casually dropped, and studied it closely. 'Nice drawing,' she said.

'Thank you. You into art, officer?'

'Not sure I know enough about it to know whether I like it or not half the time,' Tracy replied.

Tracy's eyes lingered over the sketch for a little longer, before returning it to its owner.

'Second thoughts,' she said. 'I won't have that coffee. I promised to pop in on the deputy head and I'm already running late.'

'Another time then. Now I've officially ben told I can leave, I'll get on with my packing.'

'I'll let myself out, shall I?' Tracy said.

* ★ ★

Something in one of Saskia Kennedy's sketches had unsettled Tracy. It was playing on her mind still. She'd been tempted to accept the coffee she'd been offered — almost convinced herself that staying longer would somehow lift the fog.

But she was right to come away when she did. Sometimes distance was exactly what was needed. *Watch and wait.* Hadn't she spoken those very words to young Gary, the station's rookie cop, only the other night, when they'd come across Luke Drew in his cups, communing with the stars down on the beach?

Luke Drew. Now there was another puzzle. It had been a shock for both of them when she opened the front door of the headmaster's cottage and found him standing there last night. Seeing him down on the beach the other evening, she'd had him down as just another posh kid out on the lash. It wasn't until he demanded to know what she was doing in his house that the penny dropped and she realised that this was Mason Drew's son, and that she was going to have to explain to him that his father had been shot and killed.

She'd done it in textbook style — DI Kevin Platt would have been proud of her. As she revealed the details to an ever more disbelieving and horrified Luke, she tracked his changing expression closely for any hint that he was play-acting.

Sooner or later, she — or more likely the DI — was going to have to put this young man in an interview room and ask him where he'd been all day. It wasn't unknown for boys to murder their fathers, even nicely brought up ones. It was always best to keep an open mind.

Her phone rang. It was the DI.

'I've had that deputy head on the blower,' he said. 'About Mrs Drew. Have you spoken to her yet?'

'Hardly. She's been out of it most of the time. Didn't even mention she had a son, if you remember.'

There was silence while the DI considered this. Then he spoke.

'Yeah. The son. That's another thing. I

179

got your message he'd turned up at last. But I've had another one since. From his roommate. Two things. Might be connected. One — he's saying Luke Drew came in drunk the night before last.'

'And the other?' Tracy struggled to maintain a neutral tone.

'That when his alarm went off at six-thirty yesterday morning, there was no sign of the lad. And we know he wasn't in school all day. Luke Drew's got to be a suspect, Tracy. I want you in on the interview.'

'Right.' She mulled it over. It was no use. She was going to have to come clean about her previous dealings with Mason Drew's son. 'But I think there's something I need to tell you first, sir,' she said.

'*You did what? Let him off with a warning!*' he yelled, when — albeit by a circuitous route — she reached the end of her story. She could practically feel the heat coming over the phone.

'I didn't think anything of it, sir. Just some kid who'd got hold of some cheap booze. He wasn't causing any trouble.'

'And you didn't consider escorting this

young man back home, officer?'

It was officer now, was it? Things were looking bad.

'No, sir,' she said. 'I would have done. Only we got this call. All hands on deck. It had kicked off up on the estate.'

A memory scratched at her brain. Why now, when she'd mentioned the notorious Lighthouse Estate to the boss? Immediately, she put it to one side. She could only concentrate on one thing at a time and right now she needed her wits about her unless she wanted to find herself on a disciplinary charge.

'A fine example to set a new recruit like Gary.' The DI had found his normal speaking voice again. He sounded calmer. Like he'd come to terms with the fact that she was a total and complete idiot.

Tracy breathed a sigh of relief. 'Do you still want me in on his interview?' She dared to ask.

'Yes. The boy's on his way down to the station in a car. Should be here in ten. We'll put him in the soft interview room and make him sweat a while. I want you to talk to Lynda Drew then get yourself

181

down here, all right?'

'Right, sir.'

'We can't rule her out either. Not after what Alasdair Craig said.'

'Which was?' Tracy was curious to know more.

'Just that when he rang her yesterday to ask to speak to the headmaster, she said she had no idea where he was.'

'Hardly grounds for suspicion, is it?' Tracy said. 'He just likes the sound of his own voice, that one. Unless he's cleverer than that and he's stirring things up for her to throw us off his scent. Can't be much fun playing second fiddle to a man like Mason Drew.'

'Nah. He's definitely in the clear. Checked him out myself. Bit of an old woman, but no killer.'

Tracy didn't think the DI was being very fair to old women. She'd known a few in her time — her gran and her Great-auntie Irene among them — and they were all a damn sight feistier than Alasdair Craig.

'It was just a couple of things he said made me think it might be worth checking her out. Let me fill you in . . . '

Tracy handed Lynda Drew the camomile tea she'd prepared for her personally and denied herself. How she longed for a proper mug of builder's brew, complete with milk and two sugars.

Mrs Drew sat at the kitchen table, hunched forward in her seat, and accepted it with a nod of thanks.

'When did you last see your husband, Mrs Drew?' Tracy sat down opposite her.

'Yesterday morning, probably. I see him every morning and I can't think yesterday was any different from usual.'

'Yesterday was special though, wasn't it?' Tracy gently reminded her. 'It was the day of your husband's portrait unveiling.'

'Oh, yes. That woman and her ruddy picture.' The bitterness of her words shocked Tracy. 'Are you about to accuse me of defacing the portrait, officer?' Mrs Drew's gaze was steady and composed. 'Because I didn't do it. Though I wish I had.'

The possibility that she might have been responsible for defacing her husband's portrait really hadn't occurred to

Tracy till now. It was an interesting one, admittedly. She could have pursued it. But she had her orders. Stick to the script, she told herself.

'Why did you tell Mr Craig that you had no idea where your husband was when he rang you early yesterday?'

'Ah, Alasdair. Comes as no surprise,' Lynda said, with a half smile. 'We have a lot in common, you know. Both of us sharing our spouses with a third party. In my case, Drew's love of self. In his, Yvonne's love of the bottle.'

'Where is she going with this one?' Tracy wondered. 'Might as well let her drift along — who knows what she might reveal?'

'It's hard not to feel sorry for the man. Head and shoulders above Mason, intellectually speaking. Applied for the headship, did you know?'

Tracy shook her head.

'Didn't get it. Governors aren't impressed by intellect and academic rigor these days, are they? They want charisma, financial nous, flannel. All qualities Mason has — had — in abundance.'

She took a sip of her tea and

continued. 'But there's one quality Alasdair has that my husband has always lacked, sadly. And that's loyalty. Loyal to Yvonne — no matter how many times she makes a fool of herself in public. And so very, very loyal to Mason. Why else would he go running off to the police to voice his suspicions about me?' She sat back in her chair and spread her fingers on the table. 'Alasdair's a lot more savvy than everyone thinks, you know.'

'So, you're saying he was right to doubt you when you told him you didn't know your husband's whereabouts?'

'I did it for a reason. Alasdair hero-worshipped Mason. He'd have been devastated to find out about his affair with Saskia Kennedy. Those morning runs were never for my benefit. They were so he could keep in shape for her.'

Tracy caught her breath.

'There's no fool like an old fool, they say, don't they?' Lynda Drew's eyes filled with tears and her next words were a struggle.

'My husband was an old fool all right, officer. But he was my old fool. And I loved him. I didn't kill him and I never wanted him dead. I just wanted him to grow up. That's never going to happen now.'

She sank her head in her hands. Tentatively, Tracy put out a hand and laid it on Mrs Drew's arm.

'We'll catch whoever did this. I promise.'

★   ★   ★

'You two have already met, I gather?'

Luke glared at the fat policewoman with the red hair in response to her smile. He was feeling edgy. Probably right to feel that way. He'd read his Kafka. He knew what could happen when you put an innocent man in the dock.

She'd promised not to report him for under-age drinking, so how comes they'd sent a car for him and driven him down here to the police station? Just routine, they'd said. But that's what they always said, wasn't it?

'You've no need to worry, Luke,' the policewoman said. 'DI Platt just wants to ask you a few questions.'

'About where I got the alcohol from?' The DI and the policewoman exchanged a glance he couldn't read. It made him angry. 'You know, you could be out there trying to catch my father's killer,' he snapped. 'Not wasting time trying to get me to grass up some landlord that serves under-age drinkers.'

The instant the words were out of his mouth, the penny dropped. They thought it was him. They thought he'd killed his dad. He could be here for hours. He told himself to keep calm. He didn't need to say anything incriminating. In fact, he didn't need to say anything at all. The right to remain silent — that was it. Well, he'd sit here and say nothing and then, sooner or later, they'd have to let him go.

* * *

'Kid's hiding something, but for the life of me I don't know what it is.'

DI Platt stirred his coffee with a plastic spoon, sucked the end of it, then successfully aimed it at the waste paper

187

basket. Tracy was sorely tempted to ask him if he'd ever heard of recycling.

Her boss had called it a day twenty minutes ago and Luke Drew had been delivered home in the same car that had transported him to the station. Tracy had volunteered to accompany him but the DI gave the job to someone else. He wanted to pick her brains, he said. She felt flattered. Till he qualified it with *such as they were*.

'He's got nothing to do with his dad's murder, sir, I'm sure of that,' she said instead. 'He went ashen when I told him. Thought he was about to collapse.'

And yet . . . What was it she'd read in his eyes? Something other than grief and shock, though both had been present. An emotion she couldn't name. A flicker that anyone else would have missed. But Tracy had been trained to looked at people closely.

'Is it because he's a posh boy, Trace? Is that why you think him incapable of murdering his dad?'

Tracy was exhausted. But she couldn't stop doing. She was at it again — this time messing about on her computer, looking stuff up on the Internet. Somehow she'd already typed in the name of Mason Drew.

'I have two words to say about that, sir,' she said. 'Lord Lucan.'

She pressed *Return* with a flourish and immediately several websites with Mason Drew's name on flashed up. She skipped the most recent ones, which were all news reports about his death. Might be interesting to find out a little bit more about his history instead, she reasoned. She'd picked up lots of snippets — from his wife and Yvonne Craig to name but two — but none of it was of a piece.

She skipped through the preliminary information — date of birth, school and university and, likewise, skimmed through the details of his career, prior to him becoming headmaster of St Martin's in 2000.

'Odd, this,' she said over her shoulder to DI Platt, who was pacing up and down deep in thought. 'I mean, I don't know much about what qualifications a head-teacher needs, but wouldn't you have said some sort of teaching qualification might come in handy?'

The DI grunted. She could hear his shoes squeak as he paced.

'Listen to this — trading assistant, PJ Finances 1976 to 1983, Portfolio Manager with the same company till eighty-eight. Next, hedge fund manager with Drearling Partners. Then, bingo. The headship of St Martin's.'

The DI grunted. 'Do you think it's common knowledge his dad was having an affair with Saskia Kennedy?'

'Guv, I told you that in confidence.' An indignant Tracy briefly took her eyes off the screen. 'Lynda Drew would be willing to perjure herself in court to stop this getting out, I guarantee,' she said, her eyes skipping down the page. 'His reputation means the world to her. Can't understand it myself, I must admit. I'd have his . . . '

'You know, he's not the only one with a reputation to maintain, is he?' The DI suddenly plonked himself down on the edge of her desk, cutting her off mid-sentence. 'What about that Saskia Kennedy?

Wouldn't look too good on her CV, would it, being mixed up with a married man? Didn't I read somewhere she'd been short-listed to do the Queen's portrait next birthday?'

Tracy stared at him, dumbfounded. How come he knew that? she wondered.

'*Daily Mail*, Tracy,' he said, as if he'd read her mind. 'Did a two-page spread on her a couple of months back.'

'I'm impressed, sir.' Her words were overlaid with sarcasm. If Saskia Kennedy had been sixty, overweight and full of warts, would he have taken as much interest in the details of her career then? she wondered.

'Here. Move over. I'll find it. There's a bit about how she loves to paint in her bikini, if I remember.'

Tracy gave her boss a sidelong look. Saskia Kennedy was an attractive woman, even she could see that. But personally she wasn't too impressed with her as a human being. Obviously a man thing, she decided, slipping out of her seat to allow DI Platt to take her place.

In seconds, he was on the newspaper's website, typing in Saskia Kennedy's name.

'Here we are,' he said. '*Young beautiful and talented. But Saskia Kennedy's life hasn't been entirely untarnished by tragedy.* Read the rest.'

She gave a cursory glance at the full-length photograph of the artist at work — conveniently, the photographer had discovered her at her easel clad only in her bikini. Then she turned her attention to the article itself. But something stopped her reading. Wendy house she'd called it. Nowhere to put the artwork except on the floor.

'Boss,' she said, 'I think I'm on to something.'

'Bit of all right, wouldn't you say, Trace? No offence intended.'

Normally she'd have taken plenty, but right now she was too busy making connections. *Boy At Play* had been the title of the sketch she'd picked up.

Half a dozen youths on a street corner. Drinking from cans. Kicking a football. Lads from the Lighthouse Estate. It had taken this long to register that she knew them because she'd seen them out of context. On a sheet of paper in an artist's cottage, instead of out on the street causing trouble.

It hadn't been the only picture that had caught her eye as she'd stepped over the threshold of Saskia's house. She racked her brains to remember the fleeting glimpse she'd had of another one.

That's right. The one by the door. She'd nearly stood on it. It showed a figure older than the rest, squatting on his haunches challenging the viewer with a hard stare. Darren Jones. Recently released from a term inside. Firearms offences. Now, why would Saskia Kennedy be getting pally with someone like that?

4

Yvonne had been lying under the duvet for a good half-hour now. Her nervous were jangling. If only she could sleep. Normally, half a bottle of wine at lunch worked like a charm and she'd be out like a light in no time. But this afternoon, when she'd really needed to escape her thoughts her down.

She might as well get up, she decided, throwing off the cover. As she reached up to open the curtains, her eye was caught by two figures emerging from the school-house, clearly visible from the bedroom window. She recognised Alasdair instantly. He was rubbing his hands together vigorously, the way he always did when preparing to bid someone farewell. How awkward and ill at ease it made him look, Yvonne thought, surprising herself at such an unaccustomed rush of tenderness.

She immediately recognised the second figure as the policewoman with the Titan hair, who seemed to have taken against her on their last meeting. Just what were the two of them in such cahoots about?

When the policewoman suddenly transferred her gaze upwards, Yvonne dodged out of sight behind the curtain. She held herself stock-still, holding her breath for a count of twenty. Then, plucking up courage, she took another peep.

Her next glance revealed that the two had parted company. In a flash, she was down the stairs, almost falling into Alasdair's arms as she opened the front door in her rush to greet him.

'Yvonne! What on earth's the matter! You look . . .'

'That policewoman! What did she want?'

'Nothing,' replied a winded Alasdair. 'Only to say she hopes they aren't disturbing school routine too much.'

Yvonne eyed him suspiciously. 'Are you sure that's all? Did she ask about me? Did you say anything?'

'For goodness' sake, let me get inside. Have you been drinking?'

Alasdair made his way to the living room with Yvonne in hot pursuit. Once there, he threw himself on to the settee and kicked off his shoes with a sigh of relief. Immediately, Yvonne threw herself down next to him and grabbed his arm. Unable to contain herself a moment longer, she spilled out the words she'd been longing to get off her chest for the past twenty-four hours.

'It was me, Alasdair. I did it.'

The first thing that occurred to Alasdair was that she'd drunk the half bottle of wine that had been intended for tonight's lamb casserole. But this was such a regular occurrence that it was hardly grounds for such a dramatic confession.

There was only one thing that could possibly prompt such a show of histrionics. He began to feel nauseous.

'You?'

'Yes,' she breathed. 'Me. It was stupid. I was drunk. But I did it for you, Alasdair.'

Throwing off her arm, he leaped up from the settee, his blood pumping in his ears.

'What do you mean, you did it for me?'

'It was the Christmas party. Remember? How could you forget? I humiliated you, flirting with Mason so shamelessly, right in front of your eyes.'

Alasdair held himself stiffly, as a crazy kind of protection from the memory. Why bring that up now? Just when he'd almost succeeded in forgetting. Mason, peeling his wife's arms from his body as if she were some unspeakable bit of detritus.

He could have hit Mason himself there and then. Only that would have made things worse. Far better to pretend that he'd seen nothing from his corner of the room. Yes, he'd been humiliated all right. All this time he'd thought that Yvonne must have been too drunk to notice. How wrong he'd been.

'You killed Mason?' The words came out barely audible. 'But you don't even know how to shoot.'

Yvonne's response was the last he would have expected. Her eyes widened and she began to giggle.

'I didn't kill him, Alasdair. Of course I didn't What do you take me for?'

'But you said . . . '

'The portrait. I meant the portrait. *That* was me. Oh, God, you didn't think

. . . You *did*, didn't you?' Now she'd started, she couldn't stop giggling.

Alasdair looked on, unable to gather his thoughts. What she'd done was bad enough, of course, but, compared to what he'd first thought, it was a minor infraction of the rules.

How could he possibly have thought his wife was a killer? The only person she'd ever done any real harm to was herself with her stupid drinking. Suddenly, the thought that this was so made him feel sadder than he'd ever felt in his life till now. Yvonne had destroyed a canvas. Was she hell bent of destroying their marriage, too?

'I'm giving you an ultimatum. If you want to save our marriage, you are going to have to stop drinking. Or I swear I'll go straight to the police with this.'

★　★　★

Tracy's conscience was telling her that, before setting off on her own to the Lighthouse Estate, she really ought to think about having a chat with the DI about what was on her mind. But he wasn't

198

picking up his phone for one thing. And for the other, and this was the main reason, she was annoyed with him.

Between sweet-talking Mr Chips and his merry band of housemasters and reassuring worried parents that there was absolutely no need for them to take their precious Tarquins or Borises out of school while they were investigating the headmaster's murder — not to mention dodging reporters and making cups of tea for poor Mrs Drew — Tracy had had enough.

She was a police officer, not a nursemaid or a public relations spokesman. She needed to do some front-line policing or she would explode. She'd already done a bit of investigating in the comfort of her own front room last night and she'd got the take for it.

It was those sketches that had switched on an alarm bell in her head. *Boys At Play*. Innocuous enough. Unless you recognised practically every single one of the youths in the picture. She'd arrested two of them herself. On at least two separate occasions.

Personally, she'd never been involved

with Darren Jones, foregrounded in one of Saskia's sketches. But she recognised him from his mugshot, which had found its way on to every noticeboard down the nick and had been flashed on to every TV screen locally round about the time — three years ago now — that the police had been searching for a gang of men who'd robbed and shot the owner of a local supermarket, badly wounding him.

The courts had failed to pin the shooting on Jones, thanks to lack of evidence — all the men's faces had been masked. But the word on the street that had eventually made is way to the ears of some in the force was that Jones was the shooter — he'd been heard bragging about it, for one thing. In the end, he'd been charged with robbery and put away in a young offenders' institution from where he'd recently been freed.

To be fair to her, Saskia Kennedy had done a much better job of capturing the real Darren. She'd brought him to life. A mugshot gave you the features, but the sketch gave you the man in all his insolent swagger.

What was the link between him and Saskia? Last night, once she'd got everything she could on Jones, she'd trawled through the Net searching for whatever she could find about Kennedy. Now she felt she knew her life story.

Privileged had been the first word to pop into Tracy's head as she read about the artistically gifted girl with the beautiful actress mother and the talented writer father. Privately educated, and later art-school trained, it seemed she'd always been destined for success.

But it hadn't all been easy for her, Trace discovered, as she dug deeper. She'd found quite a few articles in which the artist had referred to her mum's death when Saskia had been just seventeen.

No one knew what was wrong with my mother, one interview had reported. *But from when I was round about twelve, she just started to get sick. None of the doctors she saw could ever agree exactly what was wrong with her.*

My father spent every penny he had trying to find the answers, but none were forthcoming. I think he made some bad investments and ended up losing the house after she died. To this day, I am convinced that this, on top of my mother's death, drove him to take his own life in the end.

It went to show, Trace thought, that just because you were beautiful and talented and came from a privileged background, you were no different from ordinary folks like herself when you scraped the top layer off.

Tracy's phone rang. It was the boss. Probably wanted her to get back up to the school and read a bedtime story to the junior dorm before tucking them in. Well, he could forget it. She'd got bigger fish to fry.

★ ★ ★

It was dusk by the time Tracy arrived at her destination. Lime Park, on the edge of the Lighthouse Estate. No limes. And not really a park.

She'd timed her arrival well. Had she come later, it would have been older teens sitting around on the two remaining beat-up benches, not this group of pre-adolescents.

'Gruff!' She approached one young cherub-faced boy she knew from various shoplifting jaunts. 'How's it hangin', bro?'

The boy and the rest of his mates eyed her suspiciously. The sole female, a girl of eleven or twelve, flat-chested yet caked in make-up like someone much older, stared at her with a forlorn expression.

Gruff acknowledged Tracy's greeting half-heartedly, but she wasn't going to allow their reticence to deter her from her purpose. Gradually, the boys thawed as she bantered with them, and by the time she'd brought the conversation round to the scoring skills of the town's recently acquired striker, they were old friends. Only the girl, Tansy, stood by and said nothing but simply watched. That was fine by Tracy. She was playing the long game.

Just as the conversation began of flag, she played her trump card. Had they heard about the murder up at the school? Yes, course they had. It was all over the papers, wasn't it? Had they caught anyone for it yet?

No, but they were closing in, Tracy reassured them. Once they'd found the gun, it would lead them to the killer's door.

'Someone will be hiding it for them,' she said.

'Do you think it was one of the boys up at the school what did it?' Gruff said.

Tracy shrugged. Who knew? Could have been a boy. Could have been another teacher. Could have been someone else altogether. A hit man, for instance. The boys elbowed each other excitedly and she let them chatter on about who they'd do in at their own school if they had a chance. The entire staff and most of the dinner ladies, by all accounts, Tracy gleaned.

'Have you ever seen this woman down here at the park?'

She brought a folded piece of paper out of her pocket, smoothed it out and showed them the picture of Saskia Kennedy she'd printed off. The boys huddled round to see it, passing comments about how fit she was and asking more questions about her.

'She's an artist,' Tracy said. 'Up at the school. She did some sketches of a few of the older boys who live on your estate.

Darren Jones. Gary Atkins. Lee Cooper. Know them, do you?'

The boys suddenly peeled away, as if governed by some unspoken Lighthouse Estate law that said you never discussed anybody off the estate with a copper. From the corner of her eye, she noticed Tansy strolling further off. She was texting someone.

Tracy waited. How long did it take to write and send a text? Thirty seconds? Sixty? She must have sent it by now, she reasoned. She bounded over to the girl, who was stowing her phone back inside the pocket of her jeans.

'I'll have that,' she said, holding out her hand.

'What d'you think you're doing?'

'Reasonable ground for suspicion,' Tracy said. 'Thanks very much, Tansy.'

Scrolling down to *Sent Texts*, Tracy quickly found the message, sent to someone called Mischa.

You need to get rid. Cops sniffin' round.

'Who's Mischa, sweetheart?'

Tansy offered her a dumb stare.

'We can trace her through the phone

signal, but it would save us a bit of time if you co-operated. And I'm sure you know it would help your case, too, when all this gets to court.'

Easy. She was going to enjoy the next bit.

★　★　★

Saskia Kennedy was all packed up and ready to go. Her work here was done. Any minute now her taxi would arrive and she'd finally be shot of this place. Things had gone to plan. She'd had to kiss Mason Drew in the process, but it could have been much worse.

At least she'd escaped the final sacrifice. She shuddered as she remembered Drew's hands on her body, then smiled as she recalled how easy it had been to palm him off with whispered promises of how perfect it would be between them if only they could wait a little while longer. What a sucker. A trait he carried over him his private life into his public life.

I am young at heart, he'd written in the letter offering her the commission to paint him, *and I hope you will capture that in my portrait.*

The man's desire to see himself as a young man still had been a gift to Saskia. She'd wound him round her little finger. *I shouldn't really be showing you the weapons cupboard but since you ask so nicely,* he'd said, the fool. It had been so easy to slip into his study on another day, removed his bunch of keys and get a copy made of the one she needed, returning the original set even before he'd started to panic about having lost them.

Some men wanted to be younger. Some longed to be older. Darren Jones, for one. Thick as the proverbial. Saw himself as the hard man. As long as she was willing to pay, he was willing to do the deed. *Sweet,* he said, when she handed over half the money she'd promised him. *Sweet,* he'd said again, when she'd handed him the rest once the job was done.

Luke was another who longed to be older. Besotted with her, she would have said — until this morning, that is. She'd been standing outside the cottage — after several days of drizzle, the sky had cleared and she'd flung open the door, all the better to enjoy the change in the weather.

It was then she'd spotted Luke approaching from the courtyard. He was strolling along with his hands in his pockets and his head down, lost in thought. She'd called out to him and he'd looked up in response.

Any other time she'd called his name, he would always come running over like a puppy dog wagging its tail joyously. But this time, it was just as if he hadn't seen her. He simply plunged his hands deeper inside his pockets and carried on walking. Very odd. It was like she'd somehow offended him.

Even though he'd practically snubbed her, she felt bad about Luke in all this. But he'd get over the death of his father. She'd had two deaths to come to terms with in her life so far. Both caused by Mason Drew.

If Daddy hadn't invested every penny he had with Drew, in a previous career, when he was Portfolio Manager at a finance firm, before he decided to turn his talents to putting St Martin's back on the map, then he'd have been able to afford the best care for poor Mummy.

Instead, he'd trusted Drew's weasel words. Of course he did! Drew was a financial wizard, so everyone — including Drew himself — had claimed and Daddy was always the first to admit that he was absolutely hopeless with money. He'd handed over everything to Drew and Drew had lost it for him.

Poor Daddy blamed himself. He should have kept his money in a building society, instead of trying to play with the big boys. It would teach him to stick to what he knew in future, which was writing books. Except Daddy never wrote another book.

As for Mummy — lack of funds put an abrupt stop to any further private investigations into her health. It didn't matter that the doctors said her death was inevitable. Daddy always had hope, as long as he could keep on finding the money to pay for specialists and consultants.

After Mummy died, life just got more and more horrible. Daddy stopped caring about himself and pretty well forgot about her, too. It was the end of Saskia's idyllic childhood, and she escaped to art school where she lost herself in her new life and mourned the old one that she would never recapture. Daddy, sunk in depression, lived another five years before taking his own life. Mason Drew had deserved everything he got.

A sharp rap on the door jolted Saskia out of her reverie. Her taxi, at last.

'Won't be a mo,' she called out, with a final look round at the cottage that had been her home these last few weeks.

But it wasn't her taxi driver at the door. Instead, it was two burly policemen and a wolverine-looking police inspector.

★ ★ ★

A week had passed since the arrest of Saskia Kennedy and her accomplices. Yvonne had been following the story as avidly as everyone else, both at the school and in the media. Today's story had been about the girlfriend of Darren Brown, who'd held the gun for him under the bed in her house. Madly in love with him, she'd been, apparently.

Yvonne had walked round the block at least half a dozen times, plucking up the courage to go inside. She didn't need to do this. The portrait of Mason Drew could be restored, so the experts had said, so no real harm was done. After Drew's funeral, it would be hung on the wall of the entrance hall, in his memory, and no one would ever know that she'd been the one to deface it.

Alasdair had threatened to reveal her secret to the police. Was he bluffing? She didn't know; how could she? But she wasn't doing this because she was afraid of the law. She was doing it to save her marriage.

One last go round the block and, once again, she found herself standing at the entrance. A flight of steps and then another and there she was at the door.

A man in his forties wearing a leather jacket, jeans and trainers greeted her by name.

'You came,' he said. 'Welcome. There's no need to be nervous.'

'I think you should let me be the judge of that,' she said, but followed him inside anyway.

She sat there on the back row with empty seats on either side of her. There was still time to get up and walk out — the meeting wasn't scheduled to begin for another ten minutes.

But gradually, the room filled up and the door was closed, and the man in the leather jacket called the meeting open. Yvonne, afraid to move, sat stock-still as other people stood up and told their various stories. And then it was her turn.

Everyone's eyes were upon her as she rose from her seat. Yet not one of the people here looked disapproving.

'Hello, everybody.' Aware that she was mumbling, she cleared her throat and spoke louder this time. 'My name's Yvonne. And I'm an alcoholic.'

THE END

We do hope that you have enjoyed reading this large print book.

Did you know that all of our titles are available for purchase?

We publish a wide range of high quality large print books including:
Romances, Mysteries, Classics
General Fiction
Non Fiction and Westerns

Special interest titles available in large print are:
The Little Oxford Dictionary
Music Book, Song Book
Hymn Book, Service Book

Also available from us courtesy of Oxford University Press:
Young Readers' Dictionary
(large print edition)
Young Readers' Thesaurus
(large print edition)

For further information or a free brochure, please contact us at:
Ulverscroft Large Print Books Ltd.,
The Green, Bradgate Road, Anstey,
Leicester, LE7 7FU, England.
Tel: (00 44) 0116 236 4325
Fax: (00 44) 0116 234 0205

THE GLASS HOUSE

V. J. Banis

When Antoinette swindled Margaree out of the old estate on Cape Breton Island, Margaree swore on her mother's grave that she'd win it back. But blocking her ambition are three deadly obstacles: the formidable Antoinette; her treacherous son; and Jean, whom she loves deeply but who hates the old house with all his heart. To win Jean, Margaree would have to give up the estate. The key to it all lies somewhere within the mysterious reaches of the Glass House . . . if Margaree remains alive long enough to find it!

DEAD LETTERS

John Burke

Before committing suicide, Harold Grant posts three letters — one to his wife, one to his business partner, and one to a third party. The first two letters are highly damaging to their recipients, who dare not show them to the police. But who has got the third letter, and what does it say? The recipients of the first two are sick with anxiety on this score. Thus begins a strange chain of events, out of which develop both a love affair and a bloody murder . . .